Topology of a Phantom City

Other Works by Alain Robbe-Grillet

PUBLISHED BY GROVE PRESS

ALAIN ROBBE-GRILLET

Topology of a Phantom City

TRANSLATED FROM THE FRENCH BY

J.A. Underwood

GROVE PRESS, INC./NEW YORK

First Edition 1977
First Printing 1977
ISBN: 0-394-42196-5
Grove Press ISBN: 0-8021-0146-1
Library of Congress Catalog Card Number: 77-77854

First Evergreen Edition 1977
First Printing 1977
ISBN: 0-394-17012-1
Grove Press ISBN: 0-8021-4100-5
Library of Congress Catalog Card Number: 77-77854

Manufactured in the United States of America

Distributed by Random House, Inc., New York

GROVE PRESS, INC., 196 West Houston Street, New York, N.Y. 10014

Contents

* In French, Vanadé *(Tr.)*.

Topology of a Phantom City

INCIPIT

Before I fall asleep, the city, again. . . .

But there is nothing left, no cry, no rumbling, no distant murmur; nor is the slightest outline discernible to indicate any distinctions, any three-dimensionality in these succeeding planes that were once houses, palaces, avenues. The advancing mist, thickening hourly, has already absorbed everything in its vitreous mass, immobilizing, extinguishing.

Before I fall asleep, still stubbornly persistent, the dead city. . . .

Right. I am alone. It is late. I am keeping watch. The last watchman after the rain, after the fire, after the war, I listen still through endless thicknesses of white ice for the imperceptible, absent sounds: the last crackings of burnt walls, a thin stream of ash or dust pouring from a split, water dripping in a cellar with a fractured vault, a stone coming loose from the gutted façade of a large and important-looking building, tumbling down, bouncing from projection to cornice to roll on the ground among the other stones.

But there is nothing left, no crash, no cracking, no distant murmur, nor the slightest outline still discernible, before I fall asleep.

Before I fall asleep the city rears up once more. . . . It is morning, it is evening. A girl with nothing on is in her room, doing her hair in front of a barely opalescent, oval mirror that reflects her long blond tresses. Behind her, at the back of the room, in the shadows, another adolescent is lying on her back, nude, limbs outstretched, her body sprawled across a very low divan amid a tangle of sheets. She is very like the first girl, having the same long lines, the same smooth skin, the same mouth, the same large eyes open too wide, and the same hair, hers too spilling round a face that wears the same inaccessible, forgotten smile as if it no longer had any business being there, lost witness of some pleasure experienced before the storm.

But there is nothing left, no cries, no rustlings, no distant moaning, no words of love. The death weapon, the knife with the broad, coldly glinting blade has dried tears and all in the empty room where I am already sinking into the dreamless sleep of after the destruction. I am there. I was there. I remember.

Before I fall asleep the city once more rears before my pallid face, my features marked by age and fatigue, rears high before me, far behind me, all around as far as the eye can see, blackened walls, mutilated statues, twisted iron-work, ruined colonnades whose giant shafts lie smashed amidst the debris. I am alone. Walking at random. Wandering, as if at random, among the unrecognizable fragments of what were palatial homes, public buildings, private residences, gaming houses and houses of prostitution, theaters, temples, and fountains. I am looking for something. It is beginning to get dark. I cannot quite remember what it was. Can it really have been a prison? It seems unlikely.

Yet it is in front of this distinctively massive-looking building, almost intact, apparently, no doubt owing to the thickness of its walls, which are devoid of openings or virtually so, that I now come to a halt. On the broad, deserted pavement that ran along the very high, unrendered stone wall there was a row of ancient trees—chestnuts, I believe. The window of the room looked out on this quiet avenue, directly opposite the penitentiary. To see it the tall naked girl brushing her hair with unhurried strokes need only take a step to her left toward the casement window with the little squares of glass, half-open on account of the heat.

But she confines herself to shifting her gaze from the cloudy surface of the looking-glass and directing it behind her again, her eyes a reflected blue, at the unmade bed with the body lying on it, offered up, split open, the pool of blood already congealing on the white sheet as well as, lower down, on the marble floor with its ancient black and white checkerboard pattern.

Outside, through the dusty panes or through the chink between the two casements, over on the other side of the avenue, one ought to be able to see the dense foliage of the motionless chestnut trees and make out here and there between the leaves the vertical wall of the reformatory for juvenile prostitutes. But there is nothing left in the dazzling light, no prisons, no temples, no brothels, nothing but the iridescent mist through which flocks of sheep pass in endless procession.

Before I fall asleep the city once more rears before my closed eyes its charred walls with their blind windows, gaping recesses that open onto nothing; gray sky, flatness, absent rooms emptied even of their phantoms. In the gathering dusk I draw closer, groping my way, and place a hand on the now cold wall where, cutting into the schist with the point of the broad-bladed knife, I write the word CONSTRUCTION, an illusionist painting, a make-believe construction by which I name the ruins of a future deity.

FIRST SPACE

Construction of a ruined temple to the goddess Vanadis

1 In the generative cell

The first thing that is striking is the height of the walls: so high, so disproportionate to the size of the figures it does not even occur to you to wonder whether or not there is a ceiling; yes: the extreme height of the walls and their bareness; the three that are visible, constituting the back and two sides of the rectangular, possibly square (it is hard to say because of a powerful perspective effect), possibly even cube-shaped cell (which again raises the problem of the improbable existence of a ceiling), the three visible walls are, despite their facing different ways, the same uniform, dull, completely unrelieved white with no irregularities worth mentioning beyond four openings—one in the middle of each of the side walls and two others piercing the back wall at one-third and two-thirds of its length—plus a sort of notice, pale blue in color, posted up in the axis of this same wall; these five elements are rectangular in shape and of equal area and identical dimensions—approximately (or exactly) twice as long as they are wide—but the notice is upright, in other words, it has its long side vertical, whereas the openings have been made horizontally in the walls. On the notice can be read the word *Regulations*, printed at the top in very large

Roman capitals, and four numbers in the same type—1, 2, 3, 4—in the left-hand margin, heading each of the paragraphs that, for their part, are composed in very small characters, which makes them altogether illegible; there is a fifth paragraph as well, right at the bottom, but the number 5 that ought to appear in the margin here is completely hidden by the head of one of the figures: a young woman, quite naked, her long blond hair in disorder, seen full-face, standing motionless in a posture at once supple and stiff (one knee slightly bent, the left arm half reaching forward, the other held a little away from the body with the hand open, fingers apart, palm showing) recalling some classical statue or Renaissance painting.

The immediate impression conveyed by the décor suggests one is here in a prison, the four visible windows having been placed so high up as to be beyond the reach of the girls inside, even were two of them to climb onto one of the tables and one give the other a leg up. In addition to their inaccessibility these openings, which are markedly less high than they are wide (see above) as well as being very small in relation to the room's very considerable volume, are as an extra precaution fitted with stout gratings, each consisting of five vertical metal bars, equidistantly spaced, the one in the middle being of an even larger gauge (and possibly square in section, unlike the two pairs flanking it on either side, which would be round). The walls, in point of thickness, are those of a fortress; beyond the iron bars, which are fixed near the inside edge of the embrasure, one can see as it were a cross-section of the wall: at least two meters of some kind of masonry still covered with the same mat white rendering; at the far end of these tunnels the sky is visible: bright, cloudless, and intensely blue. The climate outside must be fairly mild—Mediterranean if not tropical—for no type of glazing or shutter system appears to have been provided to seal these bays, which are open to the weather, while the prisoners are almost all in a state of complete undress and do not, to judge from their postures, appear to be suffering from cold in any appreciable way, at least not for the moment.

Closer and more detailed examination of the different gratings soon reveals that one of them is incomplete, that in the left-hand side wall, from which one of the bars is missing, the one immediately to the right of the thicker central rod; the bar is not entirely absent, however, two short stumps remaining embedded in the masonry, above and below. Shining into the cell through this window, the sun—which must therefore be very low in the sky— projects onto the opposite wall, just below the actual aperture, a partial image (about half as high) of the damaged grating. This patch of light, ruled with four vertical lines, not counting the beginnings of a fifth, holds the gaze of one of the four young women—likewise undressed—who are playing a game of cards a little lower down, each seated on a white chair at the center of one side of a rectangular wooden table, also painted white (rectangular or possibly, on second thought, square: here again the perspective effect is too pronounced for one to be able to say for certain).

The group of players, then, is situated in the right-hand part of the room. In the center, but more toward the back, is a second group: that in which the girl with the long blond hair is modeling for a painter companion who is sitting, also nude, a long paintbrush in her right hand, before an easel bearing a rectangular canvas about twice as high as it is wide; the artist's posture (ankles crossed, left hand resting between the thighs, bust thrown back slightly), orientation (she is seen in three-quarter rear view, from the left), and painted wooden chair are exactly like those of the card player in the foreground who is looking at the patch of sunlight on the wall, her head turned to the right; but one is holding a paintbrush instead of the playing card that the other is probably about to put down on the table, and her face, averted in a similar way from what ought, however, to be occupying her full attention, turns with a swiveling of her neck toward two onlookers, also female, who are examining the almost-finished picture; these two are standing slightly farther back, close together, the younger one, naked, leaning indolently on the hip and breast of a taller, more stately woman wearing her hair in a high bun and dressed in a sort of white classical-style toga, the draped folds of which fall in places to the ground. Two almost identical onlookers are to be found—dressed and arranged in the same way—in the third group, which occupies the left-hand part of the scene, nearly if not quite in the foreground; but this time they are watching an episode the meaning of which is very much less obvious: two more young women are busy with a third who as a preliminary has been tied down on a rectangular table, the white-painted surface of which shines like new; the victim (or the recalcitrant schoolgirl, or the condemned woman, or the raving lunatic, or the malingerer, or the subject of the experiment, etc.) is lying on her back along the main axis of the tabletop, occupying its whole length; her hands are invisible, probably tied together behind her waist; her legs are apart, the ankles held tightly by cords at the two ends of one of the short sides (the one nearest the missing wall of the dungeon) of the table, the square legs of which moreover provide a firm purchase for these bonds. One of her companions, nude like herself, is holding her head by her long blond hair, no doubt in order to keep it still; the other, dressed only in a pair of black satin stockings reaching the tops of her thighs and long gloves of the same material sheathing her arms up to her armpits, is brandishing in her right hand an elongated object that may possibly be an ebony ruler, or an ebonite tube (it being impossible to say for certain whether the object is circular or square in section). It is the exposed vulva, where the bush of black hair (small, but carefully delineated, as if with a brush, the corners neat and sharp) hardly matches, with its inky tint, the gold of the glorious tresses, that the two friends appear to be looking at.

Not far away on the white wall (the left-hand wall) there is a series of little lines drawn in fusain, or ordinary charcoal, or paint, very carefully at any rate, lines like those one makes to keep the score of a game, or count some operation performed over and over again: four vertical strokes with a fifth, oblique stroke running through them; this figure appears four times, forming a vertical column; a fifth series, right at the bottom, has been begun but still lacks its oblique stroke. It would be more natural, if they recorded the results of the card games, for such markings to appear on the opposite wall. They may instead have to do with the days of sentence (or months, or years) served by one of the prisoners, or with particular fatigues or punishments, or with visits expected, or with no matter what. Something more important has just come back to me: I was wrong when I spoke above of chairs of painted wood; the five seats mentioned are on the contrary iron chairs, conventional garden chairs, all curves, loops, and spirals, newly painted white as has already been said. As for the playing card brandished by the inattentive—or hesitant—partner who has not yet made up her mind to put it down in front of her companions, it is held vertically, quite straight and full-face; as a result one can see without difficulty the picture with which it is decorated: a tarot figure representing a stately woman, dressed Roman-style, who is holding a wand, or a scepter, or any other thin, long object without discernible qualification.

According to my calculations and bearing in mind this card, the tableau moving toward its conclusion, and the two wooden tables, there ought to be another rectangle in the room. Sure enough, it is merely hidden by the operating table: it is a sheet of paper, ordinary office format, lying on the floor, the very obvious parallel lines of which recede in exaggerated perspective toward the back of the cell. This sheet of paper is inscribed by hand with the rules of the game. The paper bears a printed heading: *Reformatory*, which has been inked out and instead features the words: *House of detention*. No one in the cell moves.

II Outside,
the lengthened shadow

And suddenly, coming from outside, quite close, there is a long-drawn-out cry. As if she had been waiting for this signal, or as if brusquely called to order, but with an imperceptible delay in her reaction, the inattentive player slowly shifts her gaze with a smooth movement of her head, which simultaneously bends forward and swivels from right to left, to the shiny rectangle of glazed cardboard, decorated on the back with an allegorical figure, that she was—had she been for long?—about to expose on the table; slowly, smoothly, the card completes its momentarily arrested descent, revealing to the gaze of the other three players the hidden figurine on which the outcome of the game depends.

But instead of swiftly, even avidly deciphering the colored design, which is recognizable at first glance by the bright red patch in the bottom quarter of it (like a pool on the floor at the priestess's feet), the young woman seated opposite, ceasing in fact at this point to show the slightest interest in this major arcanum that her partner has at last put down, has now herself lifted her head toward the patch of sunlight shining on the right-hand wall, where it projects almost undistorted the pattern of the partially broken bars that incompletely block up the left-hand window, the one from which—seemingly—the cry came.

Beyond this grating, what can be seen through the gaping aperture that admits gusts of scorching air from outside, or rather what could be seen if the opening were not so high up, ought in the normal way to be a landscape of ancient Greece, or Sicily, or possibly Anatolia, a gravel road winding upward through bare, arid wastes to the small, solid-looking temple at the top of a hill: a triangular pediment supported by five thick columns, the middle one being even stouter than the others (following what is admittedly a most unusual architectural model) and the second shaft from the left being so mutilated that all that is left of it is the cube-shaped base and the capital curiously suspended in midair.

Running down the stony road is a naked girl, her long blond hair in disorder, her mouth open as if she were either breathless or terrified, her groin apparently pierced with a wide, bleeding wound made very recently. Still running, she half turns around toward the winding road blazed with vermilion drops that she has no doubt just come down, glancing as if in dread at the top of the hill where the sacrificial altar is hidden inside the sinister pentastyle shrine. No, this architectural model is really too improbable; so is the ruined column, the remains of which would be defying the elementary laws of gravity. What there is outside is simply a lot of streets, the streets of a city that has been three parts destroyed, but a modern city, or at least one where the buildings were not more than a century old at most. As a result of some cataclysm—a gigantic fire, possibly, or aerial bombardment—all the houses, which were originally about four to five stories high, have partially collapsed, and not a single habitable block appears to have been left standing. Now there are only pieces of wall forming freakish shapes, nearly intact façades with nothing behind them, their gaping window recesses opening onto nothing but blue sky or other pieces of wall, and finally fragments of a number of public monuments adorned with figures in stone and bronze that now, though still stately, show only mutilated limbs sketching absent gestures.

Yet the streets of this abandoned city must have been carefully cleaned, because not a single pile of broken building materials nor even a scrap of rubble litters them. It is as if the roadway between the double line of ruins had everywhere been cleared with a view to frequent, regular guided tours, as in the case of the precious remains of ancient cities. And indeed the young women to be seen here, walking in pairs arm in arm or standing around in little groups looking up at the empty balconies, bear no resemblance whatever to wretched waifs come in search of something still usable amid the debris of their shattered homes; in fact they are quite obviously out for a walk, pacing the avenues with measured tread in the late-afternoon light, the slanting rays of the sun casting elegant shadows of them on the freshly washed paving stones. Ladies of style and breeding, they all have the same absent, vaguely bored smile of the museumgoer. Wearing long, full dresses and high laced boots, their waists confined in tight corsets, they are carrying sunshades, many of them still open despite the lateness of the hour and bearing moreover a strong resemblance to umbrellas, the material being dark in color and the ribs rounded, as if these amblers sought to protect themselves not from the sun but from little stones that might still come loose from the blind walls.

A solid-looking building, the only edifice still in what appears to be good condition, stands at a crossroads, its walls rearing up like those of a factory or penitentiary and offering only a very few rectangular openings situated very high up, arranged widthwise, and fitted with stout gratings.

Remember at this point to mention the broken bar holding the attention of one group in the foreground. Point out, right at the front, a pebble the size of a fist lying on the ground, where it casts a disproportionately large shadow.

III Pebble and stylet

It is a group of five young ladies standing there in the foreground at the foot of the gray wall, gazing at its widely spaced openings—identical, tiny, all blocked by thick iron bars embedded vertically in the stonework—and more particularly at the one from which the cry of terror seemed to come a moment ago. The elongated shadows of the five female bodies fall onto the vertical surface of the wall slightly lower down, this façade of the severe-looking building being illuminated, at this precise moment, exactly face-on by the nearly horizontal rays of the setting sun.

The group consists of four visitors and a guide; the latter, separated from the others by an empty space of hardly more than a meter, is pointing out for their benefit the broken bar in the high window, on which she has trained the tapered cane—resembling a conductor's—that she is brandishing at arm's length in her right hand, her gaze nevertheless remaining on the four young women, whose full skirts, so close together are they standing, flow into one another, forming on the wall a single, compact, indistinct shadow, whereas higher up their slender waists, their busts, tautened and compressed by the whalebone bodices, their long, straight necks, their dainty heads held stiffly erect, and their impeccably disciplined chignon hair arrangements are silhouetted in intricate detail and with perfect precision and legibility.

As might have been expected, however, one of the four is not looking in the direction indicated by the baton. Her attention having been drawn to something else, behind and at a lower level, her face is on the contrary averted—which brings its graceful features better into view—as if she were looking at the pebble resting, motionless now, on the ground right at the front. It is this girl, one has the impression, whom the mistress is eyeing sternly, no doubt preparatory to calling the offender to order. The other three obediently keep their large eyes, their small, finely chiseled ears, their red mouths with lips parted as if in a sort of childlike expectation of what will happen next, in fact their whole concentration, or their curiosity, trained on the high window from which may issue further cries, scraps of speech, sounds of punishment or violent assault.

Inside, though, no one moves; and the only sound in the silence is that of the honed point held in the artist's long, slender fingers as it scores the shiny surface of the metal in which she is carefully chiseling the long, slender fingers of the image. Indeed on closer examination the almost finished picture is not an oil canvas, nor is it a watercolor, which explains the absence of a palette as well as of tubes of paint. And the thin, pointed object that the artist is holding is not a paintbrush. The upright rectangle within which the image is taking shape is in reality a large sheet of polished copper that shines like a pale mirror, mounted somewhat unusually but nonetheless firmly on a stout painting easel, and the young woman seated before it is engraving it with a slender steel stylet. Accordingly the engraver's right hand is at this moment tracing a faultless line around the left hand of the image, reproducing with sharp precision each digit of the model's left hand.

Reversal of the picture at the printing stage, however, will mean that the final image performs with its right hand the gesture that the live model is executing with her left, the artist, in the belief that she is copying the subject, having failed to take the precaution of recomposing the lines back to front.

This gesture is in any case difficult to interpret, the model's fingers being just concealed (from the eyes of the spectatresses?) by the edge of the copper plate, and those of the image being as yet incomplete. This is probably why one of the interested onlookers, the smaller of the two and probably also the younger, the one who is nude, suddenly goes and takes up a fresh position on the other side of the easel, behind and to the right of the girl who is posing. She now has a good view—although from the other side—of the model's left hand, whose gesture she tries to imitate with her own left hand; but in bending her elbow in order to assume the exact posture she unwittingly conceals the hand in question behind the model's hair, at least as far as her friend in the white toga is concerned, who is consequently no wiser than before. At this point the engraver herself removes her left hand from between her thighs, where it lay idly cushioned, in an attempt of her own to reproduce this improbable play of the fingers, which at the same time she continues to inscribe in the metal with her other hand.

But while all these details have been changing another transformation has taken place: the model and her image are now seated on a chair similar to the artist's, their right hands lying in the hollow of their thighs, the fist covering the groin and the digits part of the bush, as was the case a moment ago with the engraver's other hand. Now only the right hand of the naked young onlooker, standing hardly a meter behind, still preserves (as moreover does her whole person) the original pose that, before, was that of the image and its model. This hand is held a little away from the body, with the arm reaching downward and the palm open and showing; the index finger appears to be pointing to a rectangular trapdoor, unnoticed until now although its outline shows up very clearly in the floor of the cell.

Unfortunately this area is, to tell the truth, usually absent, like a sort of blank, uncharted space (from the trapdoor, no doubt half-open, to the model's crotch, where her slightly parted thighs form a cradle for her hand), so that the precise meaning of the gestures and objects located in it is not clearly discernible, apparently because of the narrator's head coming right in front, its thick, curly hair obscuring the view. In particular this black mass completely hides the red pool on the ground, which is growing steadily larger, creeping closer and closer to the large white pebble, rounded and smooth, posed axially on one of the lines between the floorboards.

Then another image suddenly returns for no reason: that of the small pentastyle temple with the triangular pediment and the broken column right at the top of the hill, the point from which the evenly winding road, getting wider and wider as it comes closer, swings down into the foreground where a wounded girl, seen full-face, is running toward the missing half of the landscape. Almost at the frontier between the visible world and the invisible, in other words at the bottom edge of the drawing, a pebble the size of a fist lies in the dust and gravel of the uneven ground, very near the spot where the fleeing victim is about to place the point of her bare foot. On second thought this allegorical picture must be that of the next card, the one played just now by one of the opposing pair sitting at the other two sides of the square table.

From this moment everything happens very quickly: the pebble picked up by a hand from the floor with the parallel lines receding in perspective, the hand throwing the pebble through the aperture with the broken grating, the cry of a wounded passer-by, outside, suddenly piercing the sweet calm of this late afternoon among the ruins, the sharp point in the engraver's hand pricking the image's vulva and running it through, the model's long-drawn-out, piercing cry as she moves her right hand smartly to the center of her bush, abandoning her pose in the process, the guided tour with the little group stopping under the window and looking up, wide-eyed, the young woman lying on the operating table, freed, her body relaxing amid the circle of spectatresses, remaining supine, however, thighs just together, one knee flexing a little and lifting indolently, the head allowed to loll sideways into the spreading cascade of blond hair, the mouth half-open, while the divergent lines of the floor (which reappear farther back) now look as if they are in the sky, above the bare flesh, where the sheaf they form resembles the sun's rays, and finally, like a distant echo, the shrill cry, muffled though it is by the thickness of the vaults, of a girl in the underground chamber, still audible from here through the trapdoor, now back in its hatch.

iv The inscription

Probably she has just recovered from a long illness—she has not been told what it was, as if the very name still represented a threat—that has left her body to all appearances intact but languid, dreamy, lying supine in the moist, dry heat that is like that of fever, her burning head thrashing and stirring continuously, motionless.

She is listening to the words, the silence, the buzzing behind her eyes. She is somewhat absent, staring at the bare wall. Her first name is Vanadis.

This name is the reason why the young wardress watching by her bedside, sitting on a straight chair a little farther back, outside the field of vision of the convalescent on the day bed, had just looked and found again the page she remembered from a guidebook—now held in one hand in front of her face, the other hand resting in the hollow of her thighs—which she begins to read in a clear, neutral voice, sonorous enough but totally without intonation.

The ancient city of Vanadium was destroyed in 39 B.C. by the last eruption of the volcano. Legend tells how a sharp stone, expelled by the crater that was thought to have been long extinct, first fell on the triangular plaza people still trace admiringly in the center of the city, mortally wounding a girl who fraudulently bore the name of the goddess Vanadis. The stone was marked with an incision that looked like two nails joined by their points to form an angle of approximately thirty degrees.

Three minutes later the whole complex of streets, palaces, and temples disappeared beneath a scorching, reddish brown vapor made up of nitrogen peroxide and burnt sulphur. All the buildings were swallowed up by the flames; but immediately, before the fire had completed its work, a violent storm broke out that lasted for several hours, extinguished the blaze, and washed the fresh ruins with torrents of warm rain.

Meanwhile the entire population had already perished, killed in a matter of seconds by the conflagrating air. The only survivors of the cataclysm are said to have been the condemned prisoners shut up in an underground dungeon of the women's prison, where they were shielded by stone vaults of colossal thickness and by the total absence of windows.

You can still today read this inscription in cuneiform characters carved on the pediment of one of the temples dedicated to the goddess and left almost intact:

isosceles volcano on the line of the horizon
as at the summit of the vee of the legs the eye
black on white on the piercing blue of the sky

hidden triangle of the temple offered on the
triangles of the red easel with bright
wounds where the stylet cuts the inscription

absent visitor torn from their oblivion
she alone here sensually spending this evening
listens to the muffled echo of another fire

The unusual shape of the letters told historians that this must represent one of the last appearances of this type of writing in the coastal region, where in fact people had ceased to use it on public monuments almost three centuries before. Yet the text appears to allude to the very disaster that annihilated the city, which would make it later than that event. The chronological contradiction that thus exists between the characters and what they relate poses an enigma that no one has so far resolved.

The reader stops at this point to examine a colored photograph filling the lower part of the page. It shows a front view, standing out sharply against the deep blue of the sky, of the isosceles pediment covered with little nail-shaped lines lying in all directions, like the ones that used to be stamped in soft clay. Below is the following legend, set in italic: *The inscription of the destruction of Vanadium.*

The wardress passes over this last line in silence and closes the book.

v The ship of sacrifice

In the generative cell—where the motionless ritual of violence and representation still continues—the inaccessible window on the right opens onto the sea. Outside, the lengthened shadow of the massive building extends for several times its height beneath the slanting rays of the setting sun, falling across the wide quay and on over the calm surface of the water, where it describes a rectangle of a darker blue that stands out sharply against the pale cobalt color. Pebble and stylet lie on the ground in the sun near the exact divison between light and shade on the flat clean surface of the regular flagstones, the lines of which recede with a very pronounced perspective effect in a northerly direction, parallel to the edge of the quay. The inscription of these two objects, left there as if by chance, in the bottom left-hand corner of one of the large rectangular flagstones nevertheless has the unyielding severity of the decisions of the goddess, occult, cruel, absent, imaginary, a goddess of necessity.

But the convalescent still lies dreaming of the reader's words. On the high outer wall of the prison for courtesans, its gray flatness betraying a whole history of hollows and reliefs, the bare stonework shows traces of numerous architectural elements that have long since disappeared: ancient arches embedded in masonry of more recent date, though already ageless, windows of less austere appearance, loggias, and balustrades, communicating staircases, a door at any rate—now walled up—that used to open toward the roadstead. Here, from vestiges of a text carved in Latin, it is possible to make out the two words ... NAVE AD ...; time has effaced the rest. But the sentence can be reconstructed without difficulty thanks to the name DAVID that appears a little lower down in those same characters whose elongated shapes seem to date from the Later Empire, giving the approximate meaning: / vacant she leaves on a vessel/voyaging toward the divine azure of david /.

This David, as we know, was the male counterpart of Vanadis, the hermaphrodite god of pleasure. He ruled as lord over this population of girls, having himself the body of a woman but with, in addition, male genitalia, very visible on the images in which the god-goddess is depicted in the sky, flying to visit his innumerable brides who in anticipation of the incandescent cloud lie open on lonely couches, traditionally represented in the form of boat-beds, before the gaping embrasures of their rooms. This half-homosexual impregnation ensured—so legend has it—the reproduction of the species, but always creating only females, whose virgin-born issue continued in this way through generation after generation until the periodic irruption of enemy soldiers into the vanquished city.

A little lower down, at head height, the stone wall also bears a number of contemporary graffiti painted crudely in various languages, one of them—written in Gothic script—dating as it happens from the last war; with a little trouble one can make out the condemnation: 'girls to be shaven,' which for no reason prompts the dreamer to make the formal association: bare citadel.

She sees in a dream the girl-king descending toward her like an angel of God. His arms are raised and his hands held behind him, at the back of his neck; his bent elbows frame his face between two huge butterfly's wings with which he indolently beats the air to a felicitous rhythm while the pounding of hearts accelerates and the rate of breathing and the pulse of desire. His ambiguous genitals also form a kind of butterfly in the hollow of his thighs. The languid young woman moves her hands to her own throat, where her tapering fingers find the ribbon of black velvet tied in a bow around her neck and forming at the base of her neck two wide triangular wings, two other, slimmer wings falling from the knot. The angel, whose breath is drawing nearer, has this same black ribbon tied in the identical fashion around his golden hair, which is gathered in a pony tail, to hold it in place during his flight.

Everywhere in the calm late-afternoon air white or black butterflies flit in search of absent flowers, standing out as little whirls of light against the blue of the sky or the blue of the water. The sea is completely without waves today, but its surface is nevertheless disturbed—on closer examination—by a barely perceptible lapping that stipples it all over with tiny crests rising and falling one after another in a perpetual vertical oscillation of very reduced amplitude. Between the water and the quay, which forms a level two or three meters higher, there is a rocky strip consisting of enormous blocks of yellow stone piled up anyhow, no doubt to protect the shore against possible storms.

A little farther on, perhaps a hundred paces from the line of shadow thrown by the prison, this confused zone is traversed by a wooden gangplank leading from the paved quay to the ship moored alongside the rock breakwater, four taut ropes, thick and stiff, tying it to two stout bollards around which they have been wound in tight spirals. A curious vessel actually, it looks like a huge big-bellied scow with, as superstructure, a pentastyle temple with square columns occupying the whole stern end. The middle shaft, which is thicker than the two pairs flanking it, extends upward to the top of the triangular pediment and on beyond, sticking straight up in the air and tapering gradually to form the mainmast of the boat. At the very top is a narrow streamer that, astonishingly, is seen to flap in a breeze that is producing no noticeable effect elsewhere. The young woman lying on her bed in front of the wide-open window then says out loud, although to herself, these words, of whose meaning she is ignorant: *livid navy.*

Meanwhile a crowd of armed warriors has gathered on the foredeck of the vessel, not in parade or battle order, nor even lined up in any way at all that the eye can detect, but in a state of great excitement, it seems, instead. On the other side of the colonnade two guards stand sentry, posted in front of the temple entrance, frozen in perfect symmetry to right and left of a low door, both leaves of which are open on the darkness of the vast hall that occupies the entire building without having any other access to the light outside. These feelingless statue-men stand firmly on parted legs, both hands holding the hilt of the heavy, drawn sword that rests with its point on the ground, vertically in the axis of the body. They are wearing those lancet helmets that come down very low over the back of the neck. Their high black boots come up to the groin, which they outline as a triangle by covering the outside of the thighs up to the hip.

Inside, right at the back of the dark room and on the building's axis of symmetry, a burning torch throws a weak, flickering, reddish light on a vacant divan covered with black velvet and guarded by four soldiers identical to the first two, in the same uniform and the same attitude. In stature they are giants; or is this the effect of their solid and formidable appearance, or of the dramatic lighting, coming from a source very low down and silhouetting them in black on a background of vermilion and scarlet—almost against the light? Their helmets and the naked blades of their swords now and again reflect the fleeting gleam of the smoky flame.

Right at the top of the mast the streamer, seen from closer to, appears as a long thin banderole with a bifid end and a bright red letter *G* embroidered in the middle. This letter gives the following series, which incidentally was only to be expected:

> vanadis—vigil—vessel
> danger—water's edge—diviner
> plunge—in vain—carnage
> divan—virgin—vagina
> gravid—engenders—david

and it is easy to see from the arrangement of the consonants that the full name of this child would in fact be David G. Here is the story:

The virgin who is that day keeping vigil in the watchtower overlooking the useless harbor of Vanadium reports the arrival of an unknown vessel that fails to reply to the usual signals and continues its slow approach to the shore, driven by an enigmatic force since it has neither oars out nor sails spread. The pythoness, hurriedly consulted, foretells an unequal struggle and advises these amazons, who are so weak in battle that they must usually overcome force with cunning, to plunge immediately into the sea, an element in which the incomparable superiority of their evolutions—provided that they are wholly unencumbered by clothing—will no doubt give them the advantage. Even before the enemy ship has moored, however, the soldiers crowding the gunwales mercilessly transfix the swimmers with their arrows every time they leave the safety of the submarine depths and execute a rapid flop at the surface in order to breathe. The men even take a very keen pleasure in aiming at the tender flesh of these graceful moving targets. Wounded many times over, they die one after another. The water is soon red with their blood.

The sole survivor of the massacre is the young girl who gave the alarm and who afterwards, in obedience to the law—but fascinated by the horror of the spectacle—remained motionless at her post. Captured eventually by the first soldiers to come ashore in the city now emptied of all its inhabitants, she was immediately dragged to the sacred room on board the ship. The fate she met with there is sufficiently explicit from the fourth line of the trilogic text quoted above. Note moreover that this rape was already prefigured in the generative cell. It is no doubt a quantity of troopers—frustrated as they have been by the untimely deaths of all the other prey traditionally promised to their whims—who then penetrate by force the only prisoner to fall into their hands alive, feverish with emotion, sickened, quivering, lost. Their ravages, repeated a hundredfold with barbaric variations and all the usual brutality, explain why the blood of her deflowering flows in such abundance, forming a broad vermilion stain in the inguino-pubic region before trickling down between the thighs as was seen in the second chapter, on the picture where the victim is fleeing from the temple and running toward the absent portion of the drawing.

So we know now that the invisible side of the scene on that playing card was not simply empty: it was the sea, into which the ravaged virgin hurls herself, either to drown herself with shame or to wash her torn body of the still burning blot, an open wound in the side of the hill that rises in a corner of the bay, a torrent of inextinguishable fire, a gutted crater on a gigantic flaming brazier. In any case, like the other girls now gone from the phantom city, this unfinished victim swims too well to be able to meet her death in such a fashion. Added to which she can be clearly seen on the next engraving, climbing the rocky strip back onto the quiet quay and its polished flagstones.

But the turbid water in which the young survivor has just bathed her battered flesh was—according to what has just been said—mingled with the fresh blood of her companions, who had been murdered in their thousands in the roadstead. The fruit of this strange union was the demigod David. The rest of the story has already been related.

NOTE: People have often confused the heroine of this story—possibly because of her name and of the frequent disappearance of the letter *V* when it occurs between two vowels—with the person of Danae, whose impregnation was very different although having certain interesting points in common with this one. On the other hand many authors have claimed that *Danae* was here simply the name of the vessel.

vi Intermission

As in the center of the scene poor Diana, also called
Divana—as has been mentioned—possibly because of a
confusion with the Turkish word for the low couch on
which her virginity has just been violated, as, then, the
solitary Diane terminates her lament on a subdued note of
despair, and as behind her the ship slowly sets sail,
bearing away its crew of giant soldiers in pointed helmets,
laden even more now with a magnificent cargo heaped in
the holds, gold, fabrics, jewelry, sacred objects, treasures
of temple, palace, or brothel, all the secret splendors of the
now dead city that they have just sacked, and as too the
wild, nostalgic chant of the sailors comes through as a
muted hum, the heavy red velvet curtain with the twisted
fringe begins majestically to descend on the end of this
first act. Instead of then fading out gradually by some such
effect as moving away in the slips the grim, hummed
chorus of the evil corsairs, reverberating lower in their
chests, little by little increases in volume, swelling hugely,
soon to fill the whole auditorium, where it merges with the
applause.

One had guessed as much: that missing wall of the
initial cube that constituted the first tableau of the play,

that partition absent from the front of the scene was the gaping aperture of the proscenium in the Italianate auditorium of our enormous municipal theater, in which the stalls with their scarlet upholstery are now emptying one by one, the padded seats tipping abruptly and thudding against the curved backs, where a mahogany surround is separated from the thick, downy material by a row of gilt nails. The patrons in their Sunday best make their unhurried way, almost marking time, toward the vast, marble-columned foyer, exchanging conventional remarks about the quality of the acting, the different parts, the fate of the characters, and in particular wondering what is happening all this time to the prostitute shut up in her dungeon.

The young delinquent is still standing in the same place, near the blue notice with the prison rules on it, the five-point penitentiary code that she has long known by heart. She is dreaming. She now feels only a very faint, fleeting pain in the region of the left groin. She can hear the sounds of the city, which reach her, if diminished, through the two small windows with stout gratings that admit the air two meters above her blond head in the north front of the building. She tells herself that life is there, simple and tranquil. She listens pensively to the peaceful late-afternoon murmur of this Sunday in high summer, at the close of a very hot day. Some adolescent girls in pink silk costumes are bathing in the river, its pale blue waters flowing broadly serene, disturbed only in places by little surface eddies; as they laugh and shiver amid the splashing spray their long-drawn-out, piercing cries already sound like the dusk calling of swifts.

Still on the floating pontoon that serves as landing stage for the water-buses, crowded under a sort of portico with columns and a triangular pediment on which the name of the stop (Central Plaza) appears in capital letters, a group of lads—students, no doubt, belonging to some institute whose black uniform with gilt buttons they are all wearing—have paused on their Sunday walk to watch the disturbing evolutions of the group of girls, at whom they are gaily throwing balls of paper crudely fashioned from pages torn out of their exercise books. These weightless white projectiles cannot possibly harm the swimmers, whose cries denote nothing but pleasure. The majority of the youths sport the curious cap worn by students of architecture, a relic of bygone customs with a rounded top trimmed with a short pointed flame.

But here we have a latecomer just emerging from one of the bathing huts, light collapsible structures painted white and marked with a number in black above each door, lining the river slightly below the level of the boulevard that separates it from the plaza proper. This girl, like her companions, is wearing only a one-piece flesh-colored bathing costume. Excited by having spent so long eyeing the inaccessible bathers from a distance, some lads spot her making her way toward the wooden stairway that gives access to the water without one's having to cross the zone of hurtful and dangerous rocks heaped up anyhow along the bank to protect it against erosion. Moving faster than the girl, who is a little hesitant on her delicate bare feet, the students troop off the pontoon by the gangplank, cut off this providential prey left alone on dry land, catch her after a short chase, and surround her; she disappears in a moment amid their arms, their provocative headgear, their happy exclamations.

Visible on the other side of the wide river, where the calm waters are darker in color, is the goods station with its multiple criss-crossing tracks making long gleaming lines and its tall signals a forest of upright metal gantries supporting a foliage of disks, square or triangular plaques, and variously colored electric lights. A locomotive under steam, an ancient model with a very tall funnel, is parked in the foreground; at regular intervals it sends up into the clear sky a plume of white smoke that immediately assumes the shape of a mushroom, as in pictures of volcanoes.

On this bank, in the middle of the pedestrian causeway overlooking the landing stage and the river, to the right of the row of huts, the saw-toothed roofs of which come up beyond the stone parapet, a Sunday painter has set up an easel; a couple has stopped to look at the picture taking shape on the canvas, the young woman leaning nonchalantly (or insistently, or in sensual dependence) against her husband's hip and chest. Farther to the right two dignified ladies, stiff-backed and staring straight in front of them, are sitting side by side on a public bench; wearing long dresses in very dark colors and with their hair done up in high buns covered with a piece of black veil, one of them also pointlessly holding a sunshade over her head (the rays of the setting sun being too nearly horizontal already for this to afford any protection against them), they are talking in low voices about an impossible confinement having necessitated a Caesarean operation, which in the end turned out well. As if afraid all of a sudden of being overheard by indiscreet ears, the principal narrator begins for no apparent reason to dart worried glances to right and left.

Passing along the boulevard behind them at this precise moment is an old swaying tram that, despite the visible shocks rocking its bodywork, glides quite noiselessly except for the high-pitched note of a metal bell struck at regular intervals by its conductor. Behind that, on the far side of the plaza, there are cafés with terraces, not much frequented at this early hour. The only notable detail, apart from the four soldiers sitting at a square table playing cards with an ancient tarot pack, the only notable detail is a small stall at which a watermelon vendor is offering his wares on a rectangular trestle table covered with a large-squared blue and white check oilcloth. The stock of fruit is kept under the table, shielded from the sun's declining rays by the folds of the tablecloth falling almost to the ground. On top all that is visible is, one beside the other, a single, enormous, spherical, barely ovoid watermelon, dark green, smooth, and regular, and a large butcher knife whose blade, very broad near the ferrule and afterward tapering to a sharp point, is even longer than the diameter of the sphere, which for the time being is intact.

Here, moreover, comes a customer: a blond matron in a pink dress with a very full skirt coming down to her ankles, which are tightly sheathed in white leather boots. On her delicate head she wears a stiff, broad-brimmed hat, also white and set off with a pink violet; she is leaning with the elegance of a fashion print on a closed umbrella. She has with her two children who are as alike as twins and are holding each other by the hand; to judge from their outfits, which are cut from the same materials but designed in principle, by their respective shapes, for different sexes, one of the two is a boy and the other a girl. It is only the girl who wants a slice of watermelon, which the vendor promptly cuts with a slow, steady, precise movement, extracting a segment of about twenty degrees, leaving from top to bottom a gaping wound in the red belly of the fruit. The small boy watches the man as he replaces the knife on the oilcloth and then the elongated sphere of the sliced fruit on a little ring of straw to stop its rolling; a reddish liquid, running from the slit opened up in the pink flesh, which the vendor has taken care to place upright, soon forms a sinuous pool right on one of the white squares of the tablecloth. Then the child watches his little sister biting into the slice, holding it in both hands by the green rind; some juice has dripped onto her white dress and made an irregular stain at the level of the pubis.

But the young mother, who has noticed neither this stain nor the fact that red juice continues to drip down from time to time, soiling the spotless dress irreparably, takes her children away and walks with them, a few paces farther on, past the Grand Theater that occupies the center of the plaza, its portico with the triangular pediment facing this way. One of the columns must be undergoing restoration because it is sheathed in a scaffolding of metal tubes forming a sort of clumsy cage around the shaft, the bars projecting unequally in all directions. The mother shows her son the theater poster, pinned under wire netting in a wooden frame that reproduces the general shape of the façade on a reduced scale; written there in large letters is the title of the play: *The Birth of David.* "Look," she says, "the little boy has the same name as you."

Inside, meanwhile, a continuous ringing announces the end of the intermission: it is high time to regain the foyer, which is already emptying, and then the auditorium, where one or two laggards are hurrying to find their seats again in the sudden darkness.

VII Hypothetical birth of David G.

So now the great weight of the crimson velvet curtain has just risen slowly in the sudden silence on the set representing the vast cube-shaped cell with the dim, dark corners, the common room (also known as the games or exercise or even reproduction room) where in the late afternoon of every day they assemble the delinquent courtesans who have been shut up here for a variety of crimes ranging from ritual infanticide to nonobservance of the strict religious ordinances applicable to their condition, but most of whom must, as usual, be minors who have taken (or been put) to prostitution before the legal age, the sacred nature of the office imposing rigid rules as regards the organization of their time—as well as in all other areas—and laying down exemplary punishments for the slightest lapse.

The three groups of characters, brightly lit by spotlights that isolate each of them in a circle of white light, are still in the positions already described, having held the same postures.

In the middle, first, toward the back of the stage, under the pale blue notice with the torn-off corners reminding the forgetful of the regulations obtaining within the prison, a tableau vivant of two completely nude girls constitutes the subject of the young photographer—a girl no doubt hardly older than themselves—who is busy in front of them with a large antiquated-looking camera: an egg-shaped black box fitted with a round lens with a visible diaphragm stop and a cord with a bulb on the end to work the shutter release, mounted on a stand of varnished wood consisting of three thin sliding legs. Elegantly dressed in a sort of man's suit made of white linen with a tightly waisted jacket, the artist is bending forward to catch in the viewfinder the graceful bathing scene she has just posed so meticulously: two adolescent girls standing close together, the taller one pouring over her companion's shoulder the contents of a big-bellied water jug of blue-patterned china of the kind once used for washing; a matching bowl rests on the floor at their feet, in the left foreground, as well as a soap dish that is all slippery curves and the traditional bell-mouthed jar containing a large natural sponge; the water streams in a gleaming sheet over a breast, a hip, the right half of a gently bulging stomach, the groin, and the downy mound of the pubis, drenches the insides of both thighs, and finally forms an irregular puddle on the floor between the parted legs, this puddle soon spreading, if at first imperceptibly, toward the white and blue porcelain utensils, which soon become like islands or ships or wrecks floating in the middle of the river. Opposite, that is to say behind and to the right, a large oval looking-glass, tilted very slightly on its mahogany stand, reflects back at the girl operating the camera the well-centered image of the bather's round buttocks.

Right at the front, in the left-hand part of the frame, a second spot of bright light similarly links three other female characters, including in particular the young prisoner lying naked on a kind of surgical table, elliptical in shape and fitted with a central foot that flares toward the bottom to form a wide circular base. The whole thing is painted a dazzling white. The girl is lying on her back but propped up slightly on one side by her right hip, which makes her even more exposed to view; she is asleep, no doubt, because her eyelids are shut, her mouth half-open, and her head thrown back in the curly disorder of her dark-brown hair, which is undone and appears to cushion her half-bent left arm while her other arm is stretched out, supporting in midair a hand with exceptionally slender fingers, the middle one bearing a bulky ring in such a way that the light falls full on its jewel: a red stone, oval in shape and forming a big bulge incised with the letter *V*. The legs are apart, as has been mentioned, and the knees softened by a slight flexing, the left one vaguely raised, the right on the contrary resting on the tabletop a little to one side.

Watching the sleeper from a few paces away in the direction of the outstretched hand with the ring are two girls. They are close enough together for one to assume that they are conversing in lowered voices or at least exchanging a few short sentences. Their costumes have already been described minutely: a piece of white material draped Roman-style (as a toga, leaving one bare shoulder and an arm exposed) for the one with the raven hair, and for the other—blond with red highlights—long gloves of thin black leather reaching up above the elbow, with stockings of the same material and color that stop at mid-thigh, this to the exclusion of any other clothing.

The third group, situated on the extreme right of the stage, is familiar: two opposing pairs of partners who are still involved in their slow card game, sitting stiffly round a circular table, an ordinary garden table of perforated sheet metal, its innumerable little round holes describing a motif that is difficult to make out, large numbers of playing cards lying face down on top of it. The player on the left, in other words the one who, seen in profile, has her back to the previous scene, is pointing with her right hand at the middle of the table where a single card has just this minute been turned up by her, in full view of everybody, in the glare of the converging spotlights, at an exactly equal distance from the four prisoners whose eyes are identically fixed upon this unexpected figure that must reopen the question of the outcome of the game.

It is a naively drawn picture of a tall, solidly built tower flaring at its base in a gigantic blaze as if the very stone were on fire, while right at the top, on the narrow circular balcony, a young woman holding her two children by the hand is anxiously scanning the horizon of the sea, apparently still looking to it for assistance at this eleventh hour. It is soon clear on closer examination that the little boy and the little girl are alike in every feature, as twins are (this was only to be expected), there being little to distinguish them in fact beyond their costumes, which custom has assigned to different sexes.

The children stand flanking their mother, listening with studious attention, scared stiff of missing a single detail, to her explanations concerning the topography of the landscape spread out at their feet: the indentation of the bay, the old districts with their winding alleys, the black mass of the ancient prison surmounted by its cupolas, a graceless building whose disproportionate size stands out with striking clarity when viewed from a distance, whereas seen from below it never succeeds—no matter what angle one approaches it from—in emerging from the various buildings that have been put up against all sides of it over the centuries, except of course for the bare wall overlooking the harbor, long since disused, where the quay, which the equinoctial storms make more impassable year by year, now rules out all promenading; closer to, at an angle of depression of about forty-five degrees, there is a clear view of the triangular plaza with the enormous municipal theater looking crushed under its lead dome, an adulterated replica of the ruined temple, now gone, that once stood at the top of the hill.

To enable her son to look over the stone parapet, which is too high for him, and see the houses in the immediate vicinity, or at least their mansard roofs covered with half-round tiles (the kind known as Roman tiles), as well as, vertically downward, right against the vertiginous wall, the blackish rocks (piled-up lava, perhaps?) forming the foundation of this watchtower whose three hundred and thirty-three steps—difficult to negotiate on account of their abnormal height and poor state of preservation—they have climbed at the end of their Sunday outing, Mrs. Hamilton lets go of the little girl's hand, grasps the boy under the arms with both of hers, and lifts him up above the granite rim, gradually leaning the little body out over the abyss.

The child does not move for a moment, possibly paralyzed with vertigo, or simply afraid that he may slip from his mother's hands if he attempts a clumsy gesture. Then, very slowly, he stretches his left arm out in front of him, opens his fingers, and drops a signal-object into the void, a thing that he made himself for this purpose and that he has been hiding up to now in his free hand, which is astonishing in view of the smallness of the hand and the relative bulkiness of the spherical pebble, wrapped in a sheet of white paper torn from a school exercise book, whose fall he now follows with his eyes in order to check the height of the building, having already measured this from the number of steps. There is probably something written on the page, which is cross-ruled with thin blue lines, but the text is on the inside and no one, for the moment, can read what it says.

This is where the descent begins. The tour of the city is at an end. Mrs. Hamilton, who cannot have observed her son's stratagem, takes one small hand in each of hers—the boy's right hand and the girl's left—and firmly leads the twins, Deana and David, away. And after that it is the same scenes all over again, gone through in the reverse order this time and at a very much quicker pace: the spiral staircase of a kind to make one scream with terror, like in those nightmares where one misses ten or twelve steps at a time, the track that keeps turning back on itself through the building in course of demolition that has to be traversed from top to bottom following a complicated itinerary that one is in perpetual fear of losing, the long sloping corridor with its row of little windows placed very far apart—but at constant intervals—through which the three survivors cannot help glancing as they pass, astonished to find themselves at such a height still in relation to the different spectacles offered them; there is the window with a view of the round hill with its zigzag path snaking down toward the concave beach; there is the one framing the loop of the river, the landing stage for the little steamers, and the plumes of white smoke indicating the goods station in the distance; and there is the one where the recess is barred with five vertical iron stanchions, the one looking straight onto the stage of the theater where, beneath the spotlights, the three groups of actresses are in position for the start of the performance as, just at this moment, right in the background, the curtain slowly opens on the auditorium with its three thousand seats occupied by three thousand motionless spectators whose rows of faces form lighter patches in the darkness, the thousands of mouths uttering at this point an "ah" of amazement, or admiration, or expectation fulfilled, like a powerful if still pent-up sufflation.

The descent, however, continues without a pause, and now comes the huge hall of the museum with its historical or natural-science collections: a boat-bed painted black, its still-downy upholstery marked in the middle with a large reddish stain, various fragments of eruptive rock ranging from basalt to pumice, an iron cage of the type normally used to transport wild animals, an umbrella, a wicker basket, a bowler hat, a damaged man's bicycle the front wheel of which is twisted into a sort of loose figure eight, a wall trophy with, arranged in arcs, hunting knives, daggers, lancets and scalpels, etc.

Walking faster and faster all the time they finally enter the initial cell itself, now emptied of its characters but with the easels and operating tables still in place, unless what we have here is a clever reproduction for teaching purposes. The heavy trapdoor, removed from its hatch, gives them access to the steep, damp, slippery ladder and the execution cellar where, at the exact moment of their arrival, the dim yellow light goes out, almost before the guide has said the last word: "the Caesarean." Nevertheless the little boy had had time to notice the reddish brown fresco, faded and eroded with the years, that is painted on the back wall; it would have needed closer and more leisured examination to understand what it represented; and that, now, is impossible.

Thirty years later the same David, grown to adulthood, dreams several times in succession, night after night, that he is climbing the endless staircase of some vast abandoned dwelling. The dream unfolds in exactly the same way each time, down to the smallest details, marked by the same halts, bifurcations, sudden breaks and resumptions. This bothers him a great deal during the three weeks in which the play is in rehearsal. Standing in the foyer of the theater on the night of the dress rehearsal, he recounts the dream to a friend during the intermission. And when the curtain goes up again afterwards he notices for the first time the altered letter on the streamer flying from the ship of sacrifice. He tries to consult the program, recalling that its frontispiece is a photograph of this set, but it is too dark to make out the inscription. So he watches once more the scene of the clandestine message and notes that the young actress is still just as clumsy with paper, pebble, and stylet. He is in a hurry to rediscover, outside, the lengthened shadow. But he has to wait until everything is motionless again, the cycle as a whole having been closed by a specious, nonrecurring, descending movement in the generative cell.

SECOND SPACE

Ascending rehearsals
for a
motionless dwelling

It is morning, very early, but inside the large empty house it is already warm, particularly as one climbs toward the upper floors where the sun's rays are concentrated all through the scorching afternoons of midsummer. The house looks inhabited, judging at least by the articles of female clothing hung as if in haste on the coatstands in the hall, but all is silence. And the whole place seems deserted: the immense wooden staircase with its monumental banister, the first-floor gallery, the intricate corridors of the second floor, the successive rooms whose doors David H. throws open one after another, he too making no sound, as if hoping to catch someone just waking up, or drowsing in a world still peopled by airy phantoms, delicate silhouettes in long voile dresses and hats with broad translucent brims who glide softly through the gray meadows iridescent with dew, imperceptible droplets of dew lining each blade of grass and shining against the light of the low-slanting morning sun, warm already though hardly higher than the crest of the gentle slope up which the narrow path leads to the house. The worn rope sandals D.H. is wearing are soundless on the beaten earth of the path, soundless too as he steps over the threshold, pushing open—just enough for him to pass through—the heavy door he finds ajar, soundless as he crosses the deserted hall, soundless climbing the short straight flights of the wooden staircase, soundless still as D.H. opens the door of a room and stands in the embrasure, having pushed the leaf through half its arc. Like all the other rooms in the house it looks inhabited, looks at least as if it were inhabited not long ago: an unmade bed, its tangled sheets seemingly pushed back a moment before the young sleeper, only recently emerged from dreams that seem to linger on in drowsiness she is reluctant to shake off as her bare feet, moving with the improbable step of the sleepwalker, cross the faded flowers of the carpet to the rustic washstand where the girl slowly pours the contents of the water jug into the white china bowl, bending over the bowl after she has done so for a glimpse of her motionless face, her still sleepy but unblinking eyes, her fine features, sullen as an absent child's, her long, long neck, and one gleaming shoulder bared by the full-length, loosely cut tulle nightdress having slipped over her skin. Then, with the same slowness, she stretches out the other arm (the one with the shoulder concealed), which emerges from a flared sleeve cut off a little below the elbow, and brings the tips of her long fingers closer and closer to the limpid surface. Soon her movements cease completely and she stays like that, her gaze dwelling unsleepingly on her slender, irregularly open hand, now suspended above the immaterial, solid-ified, inaccessible water. Some seconds, or some hours, or some years later the white hand has smashed the liquid mirror and obliterated the reflected image, the long transparent nightdress, the face bent over, the wide-open eyes. And when D.H. pushes the door the room is empty, like the rest of the house. The water in the bowl, clear of any impurity as yet, is calm again, but its surface now reflects only the tiny panes of the casement, beyond which the early-morning sun shines on the sloping meadows bright with white frost or dew where the phantom girls in long muslin dresses and sunbonnets glide with the light behind them, their feet hardly touching the iridescent grass. Inside the room, against the light, the invisible golden dust continues to descend silently through the still air, causing no more than a slight diffusion of the light, afterwards landing, at length, on every horizontal or only gently sloping surface, on the washstand with its abandoned utensils, on the carpet with its faded areas of color forming arabesques that are already unidentifiable, on the wrought-iron bed with its intertwined white volutes, its disarranged covers, its chiffon sheets. But D.H. continues his climb, the staircase now narrower and steeper. The attic is even warmer than the floor below. Through a small circular window situated very low down the solitary man has a view of the sunny meadows in which the tall adolescent girls play at remaining motionless for hours on end, their unpainted lips set in an imperceptible pre-Raphaelite smile that is like the reflection of secrets ineffably remote, fragile, fleeting, nonexistent. The corridor here is even more intricate than the one downstairs. It turns at right angles a number of times between walls of bare plaster interrupted only by a great many plain wooden doors. D.H. quietly opens one of the doors. The room he reveals is lit—back lit, of course—by a mansard window facing straight into the rays of the rising sun. Directly in the light, which is bright despite being diffused by a loosely gathered tulle curtain, is a washstand bearing a water jug and, beside it, a china bowl; against the wall to the left of the door the wrought-iron bed with its white-painted intertwined volutes is half unmade: the sheets have been thrown back in a tangle by a restless sleeper who could tolerate the excessive heat of these attic rooms no longer; her day clothes are still lying in disorder where they appear to have been flung onto the straw-colored wicker chair with the overelaborate rosette ornamentation that is the only other piece of furniture in the room. Hanging on the raw plaster wall above the mahogany and white marble toilet table is a large rectangular mirror whose antiquated surround—stucco garlands of olive enlaced with vine—was once painted black with gold highlights in the fashion of the turn of the century. The tarnished glass—poor quality, undoubtedly, since it is not all that old—frames the face of a very young girl with light-colored hair undone and bosom bared, her long white lace nightdress having slipped down as far as her waist, no doubt at the instigation of two lithe arms and two hands with tapering fingers that still have hold of the material at either hip. The girl is studying her nascent breasts in the mirror as if she were astonished by the incongruous presence of these two little hemispheres of tender flesh that had sprouted during the night, while she slept. This is pure supposition, however, her features in fact showing no trace of surprise, nor of pleasure, for that matter, nor of disgust or anxiety or any other emotion. All one can say is that from the direction of her gaze in the mirror she is looking at her young bosom, then more particularly at one of her breasts, then at the other, and so on alternately, several times, each time with the same attention and with the same slowness in the tiny movements of her head as she passes from one to the other as if seeking to compare them in volume, or in shape, or in the color of the little brownish pink areola encircling the terminal bud. She then lowers her eyes to look at her bosom directly, examining it in the same way, this time without the intermediary of the glass. After a few minutes the right hand releases the neckline of the nightdress that it was holding in the hollow of the waist, but the nightdress stays in place, still supported by the other hand. The flimsy material merely slides a little farther over the curve of the hip, revealing the juvenile bone structure with its meager sheath of flesh. And in this time the free hand rises unhurriedly to the right breast, the tips of the five fingers touching it, apparently with some hesitation, fearfully perhaps, or in awe, or furtively, although still without the face or its motionless features expressing anything of the kind. For a moment the fingertips caress the translucent skin, but only just; they hardly move. Then, little by little, the hand closes further, until eventually the five outstretched fingers meet at the hemisphere's pole, imprisoning the tiny nipple.

At this moment the face is raised again and the limpid eyes return to the mirror and the image of the hand with the slender digits closed round the tip of the breast. The hand then opens again and resumes its initial position, but in order to unfurl beyond that, slowly still and without the digits leaving the soft skin; and it is the palm this time and the five spread fingers that form a cup emprisoning the tiny globe, with great difficulty retaining contact with it all over their surface. The head, however, moving with no more haste than the hand, turns a little to the right in a movement that appears to be a natural continuation of the one before, and the wide-open eyes, in the glass, unblinkingly meet the gaze of the man framed in the gaping recess of the doorway. Not a sound, not a movement of body or face does the girl make on noticing this sudden presence, so unexpected, so indiscreet. Or on the contrary expected and in fact glimpsed long before over her shoulder, or detected even earlier by the barely audible

squeak of the china doorknob, or a very faint creaking of
the hinges, or simply by the movement of the air in the
room. At any rate she makes no move to hide her nudity
further, nor to interrupt the disturbing touch of her right
hand on her breast. Unless this apparent indifference is
the result of a swift calculation on the part of her alerted
modesty: the right hand is in fact largely masking the
breast that would be most visible from the door, and the
left hand has better things to do than conceal from view
the other, less exposed breast (it is barely visible at all
except in the mirror), since it is this hand that is holding
the nightdress around the waist, from which otherwise the
limp material would slip to the floor, forming on the
yellow paving (the only carpet in the room is a simple
goatskin beside the bed), forming on the paving, then, an
aureole of white lace, piled up on itself in a loose circle
around the bare feet, revealing to the gaze running down
the length of the body thus offered, entirely vulnerable,
defenseless, the two elegant legs with their long, long
thighs and the already rounded buttocks pitted with two
dimples in the small of the back, and possibly even the
triangle of the pubis with its blond fuzz, in the glass,
provided always that its position and angle of inclination
permitted. D.H. has made no movement either, and the
silence and fixity of the whole scene remain complete, in
the fine golden dust that continues to blur slightly the light
coming from behind, right at the top of the big empty
house, in the tranquil summer heat. Yet it is as if the girl's
face has changed imperceptibly, as if an imperceptible
smile had appeared on her unpainted lips, a smile that is
like the reflection of an ineffable secret, remote, fragile,
and fleeting, probably nonexistent, a smile possibly of
innocence, possibly of collusion, an empty smile. And
now it is her unprotected face, forgoing the rust-stained

intermediary of the old glass, that the young sleeper, without altering her attitude or changing in any way the position of her feet on the floor or of her hands on her body, by simply rotating her hips and her thin, bare shoulders, turns toward the wide-open door and the empty corridor. D.H. meanwhile continues his silent climb. Through the narrow window of a corridor, having taken one step into the deep recess to bring his eye closer to the pane, he can still see, right at the bottom, almost vertically below him, the bright meadows where the same tall, silent adolescents in lace nightdresses are playing something that looks like blind-man's-buff, as far, that is, as it is possible to tell at so great a distance. They seem to glide over the silver-colored grass, one of them—the one who has the red bandage over her eyes—with both hands stretched out in front of her like a sleepwalker, reaching for one or other of her companions whose dress she thinks she heard rustle or whose sandal she thinks she heard squeak but who has immediately ducked away with a quick movement to one side and left nothing in her place, in the direction in which the sleeper continues her hesitant, graceful progress, but the empty meadow. D.H. turns back toward the corridor.

A very young girl is advancing toward him with both arms held out limply in front of her, emerging from the flared half-sleeves of her long dress, or nightgown, of transparent silk. She moves barefoot over the stone floor with the lightness of a phantom. Her eyes are wide open and staring, an imperceptible smile hovering on her lips, but she does not appear to see anything. She is dreaming. She turns her head to one side for a moment toward a door that is slightly ajar, leaving a gap of several centimeters between the upright edge of the leaf and the back of the rebate. But the sleeper has not stopped; she only reduced her speed a little more as she passed, as if she had sensed the proximity of invisible presences behind this door that a push would have opened. The movement of her head barely stirred the long ash-blond curls, which have fallen back into place on the thin shoulders of their own accord, and the girl with the motionless pale eyes is still gliding like an absent dancer toward the small, deeply recessed window, toward the low-lying sun, toward the distant meadow. She is dreaming. She enters a room already occupied by three of her companions. It is a room like the others with a mansard window, open on account of the stifling heat of the topmost attic, hung only with very loose tulle curtains, their many folds stirring slightly in the still air. The sun's rays, very low as yet, strike these net curtains face-on and give them an almost luminous quality, throwing all through the room a light that is both diffuse and bright simultaneously and that surrounds objects and girls with a nimbus of misty gold. The objects are the same as in the other rooms: a wrought-iron bed with white-painted intertwined volutes, beside which a reddish brown goatskin serves as a carpet where four bare feet are half invisible in the tufts of long hair, a straw-colored wicker chair woven in an intricate pattern of flowers arranged in rosettes, and which at the moment hardly offers a convenient place to sit, littered as it is with articles of female clothing. Finally a toilet table completes the furniture; made of wrought-iron like the bed, it has a china jug and bowl and is surmounted by a large old-fashioned mirror in which is reflected a hardly more distant duplicate of the scene: the three motionless girls, the two younger of whom, one seated, the other standing beside her, are looking at the third, who is lying down.

They are three adolescents, slim, blond—possibly three sisters—who may be between thirteen and seventeen years old, hardly more, although it is difficult to give an age to these slender bodies with their already feminine curves, these abandoned poses, these sleepily smiling faces. The youngest of them, perched on the edge of the chair that is littered with chiffon underwear, is holding in her two hands one of the second girl's hands, who is standing beside her with her arms at her sides; it is a rounded, soft, almost abstracted gesture: one of the hands is grasping the wrist of the girl who appears to be some two years her senior, the other hand is half-closed on four long, elegant, abandoned fingers, the younger girl's thumb resting in the hollow of the complaisant palm below the big girl's thumb. Both are wearing identical flimsy nightdresses falling in regular folds, but the elder sister's has slipped off her shoulder, showing the hollow of the neck and the roundness of the upper arm. Both are looking, motionless, at the third, also motionless, stretched out naked on the bed with the tangled sheets. The girl feigning sleep is lying on her back with her legs open, one knee bent and the foot half-hidden in the crook of the other knee; her head is turned to the wall, with one arm folded to bring the palm under the back of the neck and the other arm stretched out, the hand dropping over the edge of the bed. The dreamer standing watching the scene notices at this point that she is herself only a reflection—hardly elongated but nevertheless made to look a little so by the poor quality of the mirror—of the tall girl standing on the goatskin rug, which causes her unpainted lips to part in an imperceptible smile. David H. presses the shutter release on his camera.

THIRD SPACE

Construction of a
ruined temple
(continued and concluded)

1 Focus

Aha! I can see things are becoming complicated. If we don't want them to get on top of us, now is probably the time to clear up a number of as yet imprecise or contradictory details, this without prejudice to their ultimate importance as regards the text as a whole.

On the first day of the second week, then, the situation is broadly as follows. The architects and the provisional administration have concluded an agreement to put in hand a vast pleasure complex in the historic center itself. The monuments damaged by the explosion are not to be rebuilt but instead carefully preserved in their present unstable condition as a permanent reminder of the catastrophe; this will of course involve extensive and dangerous clearing, consolidation, or shoring-up operations in order to safeguard the precarious equilibrium of the ruins. The rumor, on the other hand, is about again in the city—with redoubled persistency, in fact—that the police have discovered a secret society meeting on prearranged dates (although how this timetable is drawn up remains as problematical and conjectural as the choice of venue) to perform barbaric rites revived from an antiquity so remote as to be more legendary than historically verifiable. The investigation into the murder of the young prostitute appears likewise to have reached a dead end. Developing the partially exposed roll of film that was found—as we have seen—in the old-fashioned camera abandoned at the scene of the crime has failed to provide the expected clues, so much so that people are now wondering whether the object was not deliberately placed in the inspectors' hands in order to launch them on a false trail; all it is, apparently, is a harmless photo-feature on an enormous house that has long stood empty and is in a very bad state, judging from the gutted doors, the patches of damp on the walls, the pools of water that have collected here and there in the rooms. But what if it were not water? The photographs are in black and white and so cannot decide the issue, particularly since almost all the shots are slightly fuzzy. None of them contains figures. At any rate the special services are trying to locate the building in question, which has so far proved untraceable; there is a pos-sibility—one is led to believe—of its having been entirely destroyed in the disaster. Finally, scientists are still on the alert regarding the persistent rumblings, moans, and various volcanic murmurs still clearly audible beneath the sides of the mountain.

That evening, i.e., on the second Monday, I am at the Grand Theater for the dress rehearsal of *David*, so often postponed and now finally taking place despite the trying circumstances. In the crowded foyer during the intermis-sion I meet the painter Robert de Berg, half-brother to my girlfriend Djinn. As soon as I saw him I started making my way toward him as best I could through the throng of moving groups of theatergoers with the intention, con-ceived on the spur of the moment, of telling him about my worries at least.

Berg was standing by a column a little apart. When I

managed to get a bit closer, having lost sight of him for a moment, his behavior struck me as so bizarre that at first I thought he was drunk; and, on reflection, I am not sure that he was not. Issuing from his mouth was a kind of intermittent buzzing such as certain insects produce with their wing cases, these sheets of sound, of greater or lesser duration (pretty variable, on the whole), being moreover interrupted by inaudible, barely murmured words that can have been addressed to no one but himself. I continued my slow progress in order to verify that there was no one he was talking to in the immediate vicinity, but did so following a curved path that removed me from his field of vision. And I came to a halt right by him, although facing in a different direction, leaning back against the marble column as if I had simply wished to rest there without having recognized my neighbor, without even having noticed his after all highly remarkable presence, looking aimlessly before me at that attractive young woman, accompanied by her two children, who must be Gustave Hamilton's second wife. At the same time I kept one ear on the curious squeaks or whistles coming from the painter, still interspersed with muttered words, poorly articulated and much too fast, in which I nevertheless thought I recognized the accents of his native German.

I have mentioned already, if my memory holds, that Berg, who painted the sets for the play, was also one of the artists selected by the Council to work on the grandiose city center project, his personal contribution consisting of several monumental sculptured groups representing car accidents, executed in gilded bronze but with figures done in polychrome plastic. One of these giant works (they are approximately three times life size) that is particularly popular with girls walking around the ruins re-creates the tragic epilogue of the famous raid on the Central Bank: the large automobile laden with gold that, pursued by the police and riddled with bullets, had just crashed, in the middle of a crossroads, into a statue of Victorious Vanadis, shown holding a torch in her outstretched left hand and henceforth pointing her right index finger accusingly at the heap of twisted scrap lying at her feet, where it has spilled a spreading flood of gleaming coins bearing the effigy of this selfsame goddess, a river of precious metal rocking in its eddying currents the slack mass of a freshly drowned body, the bleeding, half-naked body (its still-smiling face partially concealed by a tiny black leather mask) of the young mistress who, purely for pleasure, had accompanied the handsome gangster who died at the wheel, his head, miraculously intact, sticking through the starred hole of a broken window, leaning out and looking back as if to take in the final spectacle of his love swimming in their sudden wealth. Up above them the goddess seems serene and satisfied, unfeeling, eager, avenged perhaps, enigmatic.

This subject, which stands downstage left, draws a horrified murmur from the spectatresses as the curtain goes up on the beginning of the second act. For myself, the thing I spot immediately, over to the right and farther back, is the altered letter on the streamer flying from the ship moored against the riverbank. I grab my opera glasses in order to check this important detail of the production (if not of the script), adjust the twin lenses to my orbits, and slowly rotate the screw to focus the image of the inscription exactly, although this particular problem—erasing a letter and replacing it by the one that follows it in alphabetical order (in this case obliterating a G in favor of an H)—was dealt with exhaustively back in the first novel I published.

This initial apart, all appears to be in order, and the

visitors in their long swishing dresses and pink sunshades are executing the prescribed movements among the teetering ruins, singing in subdued voices the opening chorus with its moving inflections. The graceful silhouettes pass and repass the footlights in the foreground turn and turn about: the various female couples arm in arm, the little band of girls up from the country escorted by their guide (complete with stick, with which she points out one by one the more remarkable pieces of scenery), the young mother flanked by her twins, whom she is holding by the hand for fear they may slip away, the svelte itinerant photographer shifting her camera on its frail legs from group to group. . . .

But I have seen all I need to and, without disturbing anyone, for I was careful to sit next to the side gangway just opposite the exit, I leave on tiptoe and make my solitary way down the vast empty corridors and through state apartments the size of cathedrals to find myself before long back in the nocturnal city, which at this late hour seems deserted of all its inhabitants.

And then come the dark river, the water flowing soundlessly, the imperceptible hisses, the smell of night, sleep. . . . Floating in the lapping wavelets were some rectangular sheets of paper, old school exercise book format, with traces of writing in blue ink, washed out, faded, blurred, probably illegible.

II Dramatic turn of events

Not until the next day did I learn from the morning news broadcasts of the scandal that had interrupted the last act of the performance, bringing that ill-fated dress rehearsal of *David* to an end several minutes before the curtain was due to come down. I believe I have already mentioned this detail of the production: at the moment of the miraculous intervention when, concluding her long and touching prayer to the goddess, the young courtesan drawn by lot from among the prisoners—and so condemned to death by burning—pronounces with a sigh the final word of her great aria, which is the feared name of Vanadis, a flight of butterflies fills the air above her head, countless brilliant butterflies with red wings and violet markings, of the species known as *Vanessa virginiensis*. . . . At this precise moment, then, in the sudden silence that has just fallen—with all the actors and chorus singers completely frozen, the whole orchestra in abeyance, even the audience holding their breath as they sit dumbfounded at the beauty of the spectacle—a heartrending cry shrills out, followed immediately by a duller sound like that of a heavy stone falling on the floor with its thick purple carpeting.

Most of the spectators thought at first that this yell of pain, uttered at screaming pitch by a very pure-toned female voice, was part of the play. And some time elapses, ten or twelve seconds perhaps, before a swelling murmur of confused words and various sounds starts to build up around the point where the drama broke out. In the ensuing general tumult the body of a young woman wearing pink muslin is discovered by the light of the great chandelier, which has just come on, lying across one of the middle gangways of the dress circle; she has been stabbed. Her right hand, clenched in a final spasm, is seen by the nearest witnesses, on their feet in horror and recoiling with an instinctive fear, to release a smooth round pebble incised with a sign: two lines thinner at one end than at the other, like two spines or two knives, joined by their points to form a sort of letter *V*. Once open, the hand immediately goes limp, surrendered palm skyward; simultaneously the rest of the body slumps. A golden stylet is embedded to the hilt in the left breast. Around it a bloodstain is slowly spreading through the material. Except for its pale pink color the evening dress is similar in all points to that traditionally worn by a bride on the day of the sacrament. The sacrificial crown of flowers even adorns her pretty head. Beneath the arch of her very fair hair, dressed so meticulously for this cruel ceremony, hair that no one will have let down, the big blue eyes are still open.

Although the nature and position of the wound appear to bear no relation to those noted at the time of the first affair, which is barely a week old, the investigating authorities cannot fail to draw a comparison between the two murders: precisely because of this too beautiful golden hair, because of the youth and innocent face of the victim, above all because of the weapon used, an ancient and no doubt valuable object of which it seems astonishing that there can be two so perfectly identical specimens. True, the location selected for the crime is hardly analogous, the solitude and primitive simplicity—even, one might say, the poverty—of a small, comfortless room (bare, whitewashed walls, an iron bed, an oval mirror without a frame, a white china bowl standing on the brick floor, a water jug beside it) in the rather disreputable working-class district that borders the southeast wall of the prison in no way calling to mind either the overabundance of pompous Baroque ornamentation or the fashionable, dolled-up audience of the Grand Opera House on a first night.

Despite the extreme commotion prevailing in the auditorium, a blend of nascent panic and that almost joyful excitement peculiar to great events, I manage to get near the dense throng of inquisitive spectators and even, after a few energetic minutes spent taking skillful advantage of the molecular movements within it, to slip into the front few rows. A perfect circle has formed three meters from the outstretched body: its center is the dagger, ringed with that bright red stain; its circumference cuts through the rows of seats on all sides as if the presence of those empty seats constituted no sort of barrier and as if there too people did not dare to advance any farther, an impassable distance having to be respected all around the incision, equally in every direction.

Inside the space thus left empty stands a single figure: a photographer with a portable camera taking shot after shot, pointing his lens alternately at the corpse and at the bystanders. In the gradually returning silence—face to face with death, fate, mystery, etc.—the click of the shutter is clearly audible at regular intervals. The person operating the camera turns around at this point and I can see that it is not a man but a young woman, dressed in a white dinner jacket that deceived me in spite of its fanciful cut. Is this aready someone from the criminal investigation department or a press reporter who has turned up in record time? Or is she simply a guest at the party, who just *happened* to be there with a camera?

The same question occurs to me again with respect to a new arrival who has all of a sudden replaced the elegant lady photographer inside the circle, the substitution having taken place without my knowledge while I had my head turned in an attempt to discover farther back what the artist can have been photographing in that direction. This is undoubtedly a person of the male sex wearing an old-fashioned black dinner jacket, a carnation in his buttonhole, and a garish red bow tie against his starched and shiny shirt front; he also has a black umbrella hooked over his left arm and a bowler hat on his head, both in the dated tradition of the plainclothes policeman. He is standing absolutely still as if starched himself, and he appears to be supervising a team of three young people in track suits who, working at top speed, are taking a large number of measurements on the floor and on the dead girl with the aid of a dressmaker's tape measure, one of them writing down in a notebook the rapid sequence of numbers muttered by the other two; and since none of them says at any point what these figures represent they presumably correspond to distances, widths, or areas following the fixed order of a standard questionnaire. The radius of the circle of congregation recurs several times in the series. On the edge of the circle diametrically opposite me is a group of young ladies in long black skirts and white blouses whom I noticed before during the intermission; they look like a boarding-school class, escorted by a mistress hardly older than themselves.

But I have seen all I need to. Not without some difficulty I free myself from the spectators surrounding me and pressing me from behind, silent now, rooted to the spot, their eyes glued to the measuring and surveying operation that is still going on, still just as swift, precise, soundless, and incomprehensible to the layman.

Outside I find the same damp asphalt, the mild, humid night air, the smell of low tide, the dark river. By the sloping stone wall where the ripples make a sound like a dog lapping, near a flight of mooring steps, a number of white sheets are floating in the swell. I carefully descend the few slippery steps and catch hold of the nearest piece of paper, ostensibly for the pleasure of plunging my hand into the water. It is a page torn from a school exercise book, ruled in millimeters with a margin drawn in red and just a few handwritten phrases in the upper half. I go over to one of the lampposts on the quay to make out the characters, which are in washed-out blue ink. Printed in capitals right at the top is the word *plan;* below are four lines in running hand, each with a number: "(1) analysis of the probable meaning of the maxim, (2) it is quite true, (3) it is totally false, (4) conclusion suggesting other possible meanings." Below these is a clumsily executed obscene drawing of the kind schoolboys copy over their evening homework.

III Provisional model of the project

On the third day of the second week, around noon, a keeper doing his daily rounds in the western part of the dig (where archaeological work has been held up for several months for reasons not specified), this keeper, then, a disabled sailor by the name of Henry Martin, discovers a new corpse in the natural underground chamber that is believed to have been the crypt of a vanished temple. First a hand, dangling white and delicate forty centimeters above the ground, appears in the beam of his torch, then the whole body, lying supine with limbs outflung, of a young fair-haired girl with pearly skin, regular features, and the figure of a Greek statue, aged about the same as the other victims and completely naked, like the first time.

Here too the quietness of the surroundings allowed the same careful setting of the scene: legs and arms are stretched out in the same positions and tied in the identical way; the stomach and upper thighs show the same fresh wounds in exactly the same five places, the shiny red blood looking barely congealed as if some balsam had been used to keep the different cuts at their most decorative. It is clear at any rate that things were done methodically, rigorously, and minutely. Despite modifications in setting from one crime to another and the variants due to differing circumstances, one is inevitably put in mind of repeated performances of a rite. Particularly disturbing from this point of view is the presence each time of an anomaly in the pigmentation of the hair: notwithstanding this fresh victim's forget-me-not eyes, the golden color of her abundant head of hair must in the normal course of events, as in the previous case, have been artificially engendered, judging at least by the jet-black of the short, gleaming pubic bush, thick for its size and finely curled, neatly delineated in the shape of a perfectly equilateral triangle. Yet there is nothing in the capillary structure of the texture of the skin to confirm this suspicion of an interference with nature.

Laid out as if on an altar, the body is exposed diagonally across a very low, Roman-style divan, the legs of which consist of large seashells in the form of twisted cones. At the head of this splendid example of a sacred nuptial couch of the period of the colonial conquests (which for some reason puts one in mind of a ship, possibly because of a sort of rounded prow of carved wood that extends as far as the wall) a large looking-glass is fixed to the rock wall at a slight angle, occupying the whole of the rest of its height. This mirror is arranged in such a way as to give the many faithful gathered in the cave as convenient a view of the top of the bed as can be had from the steps of the monumental staircase carved in the rock, steps that become shorter as they go up until, at the top, they are no wider than a little bronze door that leads to the upper room.

It is in this room, where rows of chairs have been hastily set out, that the commission of inquiry has organized an immediate press conference. Police inspectors, forensic pathologists, historians, and archaeologists, lined up behind a long table, obligingly answer the questions the journalists put to them. Yes, the young lady was raped, unlike the first two, but probably after the moment of death. No, it is not certain whether she was a virgin. No, her identity is not known; as on the other occasions there are no clues on which a line of investigation could be based. All that has been found, apart from the golden stylets and the broad-bladed dagger, is a piece of recording tape that was wound in the victim's hair, forming as it were additional curls; recorded on the tape were in all probability her own cries during her agony, which incidentally appears to have been of relatively short duration. When the yells and rattles are over, following a final paroxysm that comes after periods of varying length and very different intensity, a deep, hollow-sounding voice is heard uttering the tail end of a sentence: "like a mountain of sleep," or at least something very like those words. After that there is nothing on the tape but the crystalline sound of the drops of water that are clearly audible throughout the recording. No, there is no dripping water in the crypt; the walls and floor are completely dry.

On the basis of the topographical data supplied by the three points at which the three successive sacrifices took place the criminal investigation department's team of professional surveyors has no difficulty in establishing on the map the existence of a fourth location, which is the fourth vertex of a perfect square. They further ascertain that the center of this square is occupied exactly by the old lookout tower, now converted into a museum of machinery, which has been mentioned in the text several times already. The investigating officers immediately recognize this as the initial generative sketch. So they hurry to the missing spot pinpointed by their calculations and are hardly surprised to find there an enormous, semi-derelict, three-storied pile that must obviously be the house the inspectors have been looking for for so long, the one photographed on the roll of underdeveloped film found abandoned in the bottom of an empty white china water jug in the room of the first murder.

On the ground floor of this building is an off-the-peg dress shop specializing in weddings. The outside is almost intact: an austere front of black-painted woodwork (four pilasters with vertical fluting surmounted by a pediment in the shape of a low triangle) with two matching windows separated by the door. The window on the right is empty. In the one on the left stand two life-sized dummies: a young, barely nubile bride in a long white silk dress, tulle veil, and wreath of orange blossom who is resting a timid hand on the sleeve of a man older than herself, dressed in tails with patent-leather shoes and a blood-red bow tie but wearing, instead of the regulation top hat, a bowler, the rustic aspect of which is further accentuated by an enormous umbrella that he is holding open above their heads. It is with the same arm, his right, that he is also supporting the exiguous weight of his companion; his left hand grasps the handle of a wicker basket filled with a quantity of very large round fruit, difficult to identify because they are artificial and a dubious imitation but vaguely resembling watermelons. The whole arrangement of costumes and properties is quite dusty and the floor around the couple is strewn with papers of various kinds. There is even an overturned pot of red paint, the contents of which have spilt out to form a large pool with splash marks around it in which the husband appears to be floundering as in a sea of mud on a rainy day. A spot of the same paint has also soiled the once immaculate dress at groin height. In the center of the triangle the word

HYMEN does duty for a sign, and written in white-enamel characters on the glass door is the name of the firm: David and Company, of which the final letter is missing, leaving a gap that would appear too large for it.

The large pane on the right-hand side has been broken by an object hurled violently through it, leaving a neat round hole surrounded by a large number of radial cracks forming a star. I now notice the smooth pebble, in color like a dark basalt, that is clearly visible inside the window against the grayish floor of this square, completely bare space designed to accommodate other wax figures, brides or first communicants, but henceforth containing only a doll sprawled in one corner, pink dress torn from top to bottom, one shoe off, underclothing in shreds. Depressing the handle of the door, which opens without the least difficulty, I see that my right hand is still dirty and that I am going to have to wash it once more.

In the back of the shop, which has been virtually cleared of its furniture, the only thing left is an old garden table with a perforated top representing by means of a subtle arrangement of holes and solid areas two children playing cards, seated opposite each other on either side of a very similar table. I search for a moment among the litter of papers in the window containing the newlyweds, no doubt in the secret hope of laying my hands on some message; but burrow as I may in the mass of scattered documents I can find no inscription worth reporting; apart from the newspaper cuttings relating to news items of more or less recent date there are above all sheets of accounts bearing columns of figures and complicated multiplication sums. When I get up again, my clothes covered in dust, I find that my right hand is now in addition stained red.

A trapdoor gives access to a steep ladder leading down

to the basement, an enormous vaulted cellar with a brick ceiling and reinforced-concrete columns, chock-full of ancient, discarded equipment—wheels, stands, winches, chains, and pulleys—that might be the dismantled machinery of a theater offering the more spectacular types of variety, or possibly an old piece of clockwork for operating a traveling cradle or goods hoist. There is also, in one corner, a whole pile of trunks and boxes even including three wrought-iron cages big enough and strong enough to hold wild animals of the size of a very large dog.

Judging by appearances, the first floor must have been occupied by an illicit brothel, which also extended to the second. Each room contains a simple, fairly wide brass bed, a black prayer stool, and numerous mirrors; the windows have been crudely filled in with brick and plaster jointing (so the casements visible from outside are a take-in); all the cells have several rings fixed to the walls in various positions difficult to account for. Each inmate's given name is still written upon the corridor side of her door, as is her age: the girls would all appear to have been nearer fifteen than twenty; the small piece of card with this information written on it by hand—together sometimes with other information of a less explicit nature—is fixed in the center of the wooden leaf by four rusty thumbtacks.

I walk down the second-floor corridor making out one after another of these summary identifications traced in blue ink by the same careful hand on identical rectangles of normal visiting-card format. The layout of the rooms is the same as below, the doors alternating regularly from one side of the corridor to the other, that is to say: one on the right, three steps, one on the left, three steps, one on the right, etc. There seem now to be many more of them than on the first floor, and the corridor seems a lot longer, which is quite impossible.

I come at last to the wooden staircase, which on the contrary seems much narrower than the flights I have climbed previously. The treads have been thoroughly soiled by wet shoes—men's, obviously, and coming down—that have left a large number of black prints reproducing the shapes of their soles and heels.

As soon as I reach the floor above, the destination of which is given as being still obscure, I realize that a leak must have occurred in the plumbing because a great sheet of liquid, varying in depth from place to place, covers most of the floor and is seeping slowly through to the rooms below, which explains the innumerable pools spreading drop by drop throughout the house. I decide to take advantage of this to try and wash my hands, but without success: the blackish water (from the central heating, perhaps?) only deposits more dirt on my fingers and palms.

It is at this level that one has the best idea of just how badly the building has been damaged: the whole rear façade appears to be on the point of collapsing, big cracks have already opened in the walls of the top two stories, and entire sections of wall on that side look as if they only need a gentle push to send them tottering out into space. It was time something was done. Fortunately the most urgent salvage work was begun straight away, because if pine trunks were not shoring up the worst-threatened walls the whole building would have fallen down long ago. Subsequently a few injections of plastic cement in the fissured masonry will suffice to arrest further decay and preserve the place in its present form. Similarly preserving the sheet of water on the top floor and its regular flow down through the ceiling without provoking the rapid or gradual deterioration of the latter will pose more complex problems. But the most hazardous measure of all will without a doubt be the construction of the Holy of Holies (in the underground part), which has to include a stake for the burnt offerings. At all events there is no question at this stage of reopening the debate regarding the choice of this ruined building for installing the sanctuary.

FOURTH SPACE

*Reveries of young girls
confined between window
and looking-glass*

1 Affected vagrancy meanwhile

Respite

Locked up for what fancied lapse does the captive minor wait, doomed to what fate? The prisoner of too sultry a summer of endless afternoons, she has ordained her own solitary confinement. She wishes to know neither the object nor the term of her penance. The wide-open window looks out onto walls where, falsely pensive, she can read nothing.

On the other side of her dungeon is the mirror reflecting an image of herself, and on that image she slowly watches—imagines—the budding promise of the offense she has been condemned to commit, and for which she is being punished.

The double

She who looks at herself for too long finds the glass has duplicated her. I see a second girl, the improbable lover, other, inaccessible, born of solitude and dream and of the venturing hand: twice two hands, twice two eyes, twice two breasts. Did I dream also of twice two mouths, with twice twice two lips?

Soft escape

In sleep the walls of the prison fray away into thin sheets of fleecy mist that glide gently along the ground. They are like sheep wandering over the heath in search of the lost fold or of the shepherdess, gulls soaring in circles round a submerged scrap of white, pale flowers in the white grass, or the impossibly light garments one wears in dreams: a dress of transparent gauze, a long scarf like a pink wraith floating out horizontally, a superfluous sunshade, a flowered bonnet, immaterial and translucent as the golden shadow in the sunlight.

But now outlines and solids are becoming clearer: it is me, that's all. I am outside the glass walls of the cage, the other side of the mirror. Intoxicated by the very whiteness of the air, I hover in slow motion several centimeters above the frost-covered ground, a fugitive girl going to meet my sole companion, or simply myself, a hand held out before me to touch her the sooner, a sleepwalker wandering over the heath in search of the lost house.

Two return

Abruptly the birds fly away. A sudden puff of wind whips the tall grass against bare skin under the dress and lifts the brim of the impossibly wide hat. . . . The gust sending a thrill through my whole body. Who was saying this was a dream? No. This is me, this is really me this time. And I have taken my girlfriend's hand and am walking toward the house, pulling her along the path through the docile undergrowth that lies down as we pass. And we too lie down in the submissive grass. And on the unmade bed, pale blue muslins, golden sunbonnets, white shoes, and pink garlands of flowers all removed, I gaze at the languid form of the girl pretending to be falling asleep. Again, slowly my hand advances toward the bare skin. . . . And anyway, if this were a dream there would be no colors.

Innocence to enjoy

No! That's all wrong. There are no fleecy sheep and no couple running through the meadows. There is nothing outside. And here, well sheltered, I am alone, quiet, untouched. They call me Vanadis but I don't care, my real name is Suzanne. I am naked but intact. Kneeling on my prayer stool, I feel innocent and hard. My gaze is empty. It is only you examining my body with that uneasy look.

The schoolgirl

I am a studious little girl; I go to school every day, and no one waits for me when I come out of class. I go home without glancing to right or left. I walk straight ahead.

When I come to the pretty shop that occupies the whole ground floor of the building I see Mr. David standing on his doorstep between the two big windows in which young newlyweds, first communicants, and novices part their lips to smile as one. Mr. David smiles at me too, looking like a kindly wolf. But I barely respond with a little nod before quickly climbing the stairs.

I go to bed early and get up early; I do not lie in bed

daydreaming. At school I take Balinese dancing, Latin, sexual pathology, psychoanalysis, and the theory of variable sets. And I do not look at the pigeons out of the window.

I also study my own gestures, correcting attitudes and postures in accordance with the advice of my teacher; I listen to him with eyelids lowered, without seeing him, as I have been taught to do. Nor do I look at the pairs of pigeons through the open window, nor do I hear their cooing.

Spring already too warm

But here the prisoner lifts her gaze unthinkingly and notices the pigeons again with their expressionless looks, their ungainliness, their tendency to fly off for no reason, and the tedious repetitiveness of their convolutions on the gravel: a disheveled male, puffed up as if with anger, turning round and round and at the same time moving around an immaculate little female, executing intricate and obsessive circles in a series of leaps, edging closer and closer each time he passes the woman with her sleek plumage, she meanwhile pretending to see nothing at all.

And yet again it is the same images that follow one another: the sheep with their soft coats that one was counting to get to sleep, the big black dog that has sniffed something or other, the body of an adolescent girl flung in an almost dislocated posture in the grass: a shepherdess ravaged by the storm, by the overpowering smells, by the wind. Erect, motionless, she is dreaming, smelling, listening. Everything around her is shifting: the grass, the motionless earth, the motionless lake and the still leaves on the trees, and the statues in the park and the footsteps on the gravel.

Shooting a sitting bird

Thoughtful now, the young model holds her gesture, seen as if by herself without the looking-glass, without the window, without the door being ajar. Three brisk movements would be enough, three quick rustlings of dry material—unwieldy veils tearing, the dress of stiffened muslin, the demure white underwear being ripped off and hurled with one swing of the two slim arms into a corner of the bare room—would be enough for her to be totally exposed once more. But she checks herself in mid-gesture and becomes still again as if rooted to the spot by a sudden thought, her elbow half-bent, back arched in the strained posture of a statuette, the folds of the light material fixed for one fragile—hazardous—final moment.

Surrender

Weary at last of watching that inscrutable eye peer at her, she turns away with a shrug of her shoulders, curls up, and pretends to succumb to sleep like a child. She no longer wishes even to hear the clicking eyelid that opens and shuts periodically on its prey. Absent, offered up, guileless, indifferent, she lets it—as far as her image is concerned—all happen.

Liquid sleep

The waves roll up the beach, fall back, fresh waves roll up. But the eye of the black bird (the smooth iris that duplicates the live object on which it rests), the mechanical eye pursues the sleeping girl right into her dream where, standing in the roughest part of the surf, she bathes and bathes all the burning parts of her body to cleanse them of the day's impurities. The repeated click of the shutter merges now with the sound of the waves, with the sound of the water pouring from the pitcher into the bottom of the china bowl, the sound of the hand stirring the tepid water in the tub to relish its coolness, the hand gliding to and fro over the smooth skin (concerned to wash better?), the eye watching, the lips brushing as if by chance, the fingertips imperceptibly touching the secret regions as if on another's body, or as if it were her own flesh.

II Second initiatory cycle

Pretending

If one is alone one must pretend to be two. With two, one must pretend to be three. Anything more than that is too difficult, even with several windows and several mirrors of different shapes. With more than three people it is best to pretend to be alone.

Doubtful identity

Otherwise one has to resort to subterfuges such as wigs or cosmetics for painting the mouth and eyes, or wear a cloche hat with lace and flowers, the kind known as a "funny hat," and assume an inspired, dreamy look (it is difficult not to laugh), imitating the drifting expression of the girl who has just had a letter from far away, from the Indies or the Andes or the Endies, from some country that does not exist, a blue letter recounting incredible things: the story of the three little girls living at the bottom of a well, the story of the seven adolescents wed by Gilles de Retz, the story of the twenty-four captives shut up in the underground prison of Vanadium, the one about the hundred and twenty-one underage prostitutes of the Blue Villa in Shanghai, or the nine hundred and ninety-nine nocturnal companions of King Solomon, son of David; or it might be the story of the eleven thousand virgins of Cologne, or lastly that of an indeterminate number of girls who do not exist, as pretty as pictures and whose pictures multiply from page to page of a book one pretends to be seeing for the first time.

Rules of the game

This is the list of regulations:

Two people look at each other in a mirror while keeping their eyes as far as possible unfocused as if looking at something much farther away, something uncertain and nebulous that is slowly passing without altering its position.

Dress each other up, using veils that are either too short or torn. Tie a piece of some unlikely material around each other's hips. Make a dress out of curtains.

Spray each other with perfume in all the delicate places, one after another in the same order. (No mistakes allowed.)

Read a silly sonnet together.

Assume a highly romantic expression to utter obscenities, all the time looking at each other in the mirror.

Each player in turn then pretends to be asleep while the other, having opened the poetry book at the same page, re-reads the piece aloud with the words in a different order. Both players' bodies must be touching throughout in one place only, as if by chance: the toe of one foot in an armpit or the crook of an elbow around the tip of a breast.

The text complained of is then altered again by replacing the poetic words with coarse terms denoting the secret parts of the female body in such a way that it becomes meaningless. One can start with nouns that have the same number of feet as the original, and go on with words that are much too long or much too short.

Afterwards one crosses to the window, lifts the net curtain, and looks out, saying to invisible witnesses: "She's stupid. She doesn't understand a thing. Just sleeps like a slimy plant."

After this come back to the bed and say quietly in her ear, speaking very clearly: "You're nothing but a little slut, a pool of filth, a damp meadow, a half-open clam." Then step back a little to look at her, giving her a nice smile, which she does not even see because she really has fallen asleep.

Smells

Smell a damp meadow, as has been said, smell of new-mown hay, smell of faded flowers, smell of leather boots, smell of shellfish, smell of hair, smell of horses.

One hides together in a barn full of hay where it is much too hot and dances barefoot like madwomen till the sweat runs.

Stopping abruptly to look out of the smallest of the windows as if struck by some amazing sight in the water-meadow, one says slowly without turning around: "The chestnut filly pees standing up with her legs apart."

Then one goes right up to the other girl and murmurs in her hair: "You're too hot, little mustang, you're dripping wet."

Gust of wind before rain

With a toss of the head one must now pretend to be angry in order to make the other girl apologize. (The fact that she has done nothing wrong—apparently—is not taken into consideration, quite the contrary.) Meanwhile one turns away from her and unconcernedly combs one's hair. The sly little piece is used to changes in the weather and closes her eyes to let the storm pass over. But one tells her she must kneel down and one bends her neck for her to hide her shame at the same time as her face in the hollow of one's thighs. One tells her: "You're heavy, you're all limp, you cling to me like seaweed." One takes advantage of the situation to caress her sweetly captive shoulders, which quite by chance happen to be bare. Finally, because she is pretty one forgives her and tells her a true story:

Repeatedly upon a time (in fact one could say as a rule) a brand-new little nightdress with ribbons and embroidered lace was carried off by a gust of wind one stormy night. The gust of wind blew her out through the window and under a thorn hedge, whence she could not escape because she was a prisoner, caught on the spiky branches by the neck and arms. After an hour she was already all torn, so wildly had the wind embraced her this way and that. Then, to free her, lightning struck them both, and the thicket blazed up in an instant, burning like a holiday bonfire. Immediately afterwards it began to rain in torrents. When she got home next morning she was fit only to be thrown with the dirty rags, if that.

In petrified nature

We've fallen silent. We have nothing more to say to each other. Our heads are empty. Our ears are full of the invisible buzzing of the insects singing on all sides simultaneously. We are in the country, before the first war, or toward the end of the last century, in a land with no parents and no boys, as usual.

We have umbrellas doing duty as sunshades and wicker food baskets. We are reading old-fashioned novels set in the depths of a phantom Africa, full of psychological dramas that are quite incomprehensible in the humid heat and the chirring of the crickets.

The coffeepot still stands on the table under the big tree together with the breakfast cups, the meal having not yet been cleared away.

We have stolen the voyeur's bicycle. It is an ancient man's bicycle that was left in the sheepfold (we always saw it there) and has been called that ever since a dreadful story that was once made up about it. It is more convenient than our bicycles because of the crossbar that holds the skirt up at the front and leaves the thighs free. We have heaped the pillion and handlebars with wildflowers.

We are bored. We make bouquets that fade immediately. We are together all the time. There is no more time. We have not spoken for days and days. I think we have lost the power of speech.

Then suddenly we would appear to have heard a curious noise: like a knife being sharpened, up where the road bends. We looked at each other, still without saying anything. And in a single movement we left road, bicycles, food baskets, and sunshades and went running off through the undergrowth as fast as our legs could carry us. We were very frightened, apparently.

Following on as usual are a vertiginous staircase and a long corridor, with blood coming out under the door of a locked room. And the same dreadful story starts all over again, dreamt in the shade of the great, motionless tree.

Demon drowsing

She cried out in her sleep. It was like a yell of terror that, getting caught in her throat, turned into a kind of repeated rattle, a long-drawn-out, plaintive sound rising and falling with more volume or less as dictated by a groundswell emerging from the burning depths. Taking and holding her hand is not enough to wrest her from the panic fear of the flooded cave that is sucking her down with it. The seventh wave is stronger and draws a groan of pain. She needs rougher treatment, needs to be seized by the shoulders, stood up, slapped, shaken like a rag doll. The dislocated pieces of the nightmare come away from her one by one and fall at her feet like incomprehensible ribbons of clothing.

Half-awake at last, she catches sight of her nakedness in the rectangular looking-glass above the divan on which she had dozed off, and she hardly recognizes herself. She is still dreaming, supine in the grass, exposed, offered up, legs flung out and hands held together behind her neck, amid the cushions beneath the big, motionless, probably baleful mirror, a prisoner of her phantoms who has fallen asleep in her own arms.

To rid her of the incubal caresses still lingering here and there on her young skin, to remove the dust of the road, the beads of dew, the scraps of undergrowth or faded flowers caught in her secret tufts, her body must now be washed with water from the spring gathered in full sunlight, for there is no trusting that from the well, which is too deep. She whimpers a little as the long torrents stream all over her. Is she quite clean again, innocent and pure for the sacrifice? A careful search is carried right into the sinful recesses for any suspicious traces the demon may have left there.

She lets it all happen. She no longer says anything. She is absent. Soon she will fall asleep again.

Metamorphosis and assumption

What does she do, however, but turn into a dove once more: hardly was one's back turned before the big white features were sprouting and fanning out in the light. . . . It's too irritating, it really is! But one has a definite feeling of having spotted the mark of the beast on her left breast, just outside the areola; and again she is pretending to be an angel from heaven. Now she even takes off, her heavy, lavish wings beating the air in an easy rhythm, making an infernal din.

And we two are left there watching her fly away over the dry stone wall toward the end of the meadow, where she is already no more than a cloud of reddish brown vapor at the edge of the impenetrable forest.

Harem spells

To console you I'm going to tell you our true story. Hardly out of infancy, we were apparently both bought by the sultan—our parents being too poor to feed us—and shut up in an old-fashioned palace full of velvets and silks, furs, marbles, and doors sealed with padlock and chain. All day long we nibble comfits, languishing on buff sofas, our only companions little dogs with curly hair, perfumed and docile, they too gorged with milk, opium, and sweetmeats.

The sultan is neither old nor cruel. In fact he is apparently rather nice; but he is stupid, like all boys, and we have told him we do not want to see him again. He has sent us a book, ostensibly to entertain us. It is a curious book, full of photographs of girls clasped in each other's arms, more or less nude, with their straps always slipping off their shoulders and little knickers that fit loosely between the thighs, the whole thing accompanied by childish captions written in a style that strikes us as being quite out of place.

Before long, having leafed through the book backwards and forwards, we become aware that the pictures are poisoned: as one looks at them one's will weakens, one's mind clouds, and one's body becomes warm and soft; particularly the neck is already more sensitive and more supple, more sinuous, more fragile. . . . It has undoubtedly grown longer too, and at the same time the skin has grown finer; it seems as smooth and round now as a swan's neck. . . . All of a sudden we remember that, on the pretext of celebrating our arrival, the sultan had all his young wives strangled, just for fun, and afterwards had his prettiest horses' throats slit.

We turn simultaneously toward one of the narrow windows of our prison, the one with a bar missing from the wrought-iron grating. . . .

The magic forest

We escaped through the window. But the forest around the castle is enchanted too: grass stems twine around our ankles, poisonous plants hanging down all over the place laugh in silent mockery above our heads, long creepers swing down from the branches as we pass to seize us by the waist, by the armpits, or by the wrists. As little by little we lose our wind in this breathless chase, the large red-fleshed flowers falling ceaselessly from the orchids that adorn the giant trunks take advantage of our panting to force their way into our open mouths and start to choke us. Our hair too, having come down in the struggle, is like tangles of snakes, and our torn dresses hang from our hips in long streaming scarves, bewitched sashes that start to dance the saraband, for no very good reason since there is not the least movement in the air.

It was just as we were about to succumb with exhaustion that we finally reached the shore.

The sea! Long before seeing it for the first time, often in childhood I dreamt of the sea. The sea is a flat, calm expanse painted a uniform blue on which one can run to one's heart's delight quite comfortably without getting wet. Unlike the water of streams and rivers, in which one can do no more than warily dip one's toes (any farther is extremely dangerous), one walks on the surface of the sea without sinking in or leaving the least trace; and one proceeds in the same dreamlike glide, experiencing as little resistance as fatigue, to the horizon, which is by no means as far off as they say.

Then one sees what there is on the other side. . . .

Love here now

On the other side there is the garden and the house, which have not moved. Right. Now we're home again. We've had enough of outings into the country, voyages, adjectives, and metaphors. We tried that for fun; it wasn't much fun.

We change. We put on old blouses so worn as to have become transparent, and we do not even bother to button them. We make chocolate in large cups. On our skin there are at worst one or two little marks left here and there; they must be mosquito bites.

We try to read one of the old books that have been lying in a corner since goodness knows when. And we find it really too silly.... We catch each other's eye for a moment as if inadvertently. We say no more and yet this time we know it has been said: we are going to sleep together.

There is no one about. It's easy. We pretend to be very sleepy all of a sudden; but it's not true, as we know very well: it's only in order not to frighten each other, and also not to be scared any more.

And afterwards

Afterwards it's much better, possibly; at any rate there's been a change. Often as a child I dreamt of the sea: a welcoming, uniform expanse painted a deep blue; the freedom to run right to the horizon. It was also vertical and flat. It opened in the middle like a double door. Now we can dip our feet in it, look at the bottom, catch shrimps in the holes as well as other creatures of the same sort that leave a funny smell on one's fingers, a familiar smell. Perhaps we have aged a bit. To go on the sea, where the horizon always recedes, we now have to take the little boat moored at the jetty, at the entrance to which that old bicycle is still standing.

FIFTH SPACE

*The criminal
already
on my trail*

1 Return erased

It is morning. It is evening. I remember.

It was humid and mild. I was walking home along the river bank as usual. In nooks and crannies always out of sight—or at least at the barely visible limits of one's field of vision—one heard the babbling of the water as it trickled along the gutters and drains, tiny sounds of breathing, of intermittent sucking, of a soft falling at the edge of the river, hushing sounds too on the slippery ground, faint slimy sliding sounds and all kinds of sticky contacts of even more dubious origin, punctuated from time to time by the sharper plop of some liquid dripping into a pool. One stops for a moment. One waits for that slower footstep, the absent, suspended sound of a foot checked in midair. . . . One listens. I listened. It was night.

Now in the keener air where breathing is less oppressive, now in the warm drizzle that resumed at intervals, I walked at a steady pace through the deserted city. Yet I must have gone to bed very late; and I slept for a long time, as always.

Just at the foot of the quay a few sheets of white paper are washing about half underwater together with other flotsam: washed-out bits of cardboard wrappings, driftwood, greenish rinds from some large round fruit cut in slices—melon or watermelon—with a little red flesh still sticking to them here and there. The wet pavement suddenly gleams in places with a great blood-colored splash. I continued my lonely walk along the canals and alleys. What with all the detours, precautions, and feints I must have spent hours getting home. I went to bed very late and slept for a long time, as always.

I was crouching on the lowest negotiable tread of one of those little flights of mooring steps leading down to the water, right at the bottom of the sloping wall of dressed stone grown green with frequent immersion. In the dim light of an old lamppost up on top of the quay I wash my hands as carefully as it is possible to do in this dark, murky water littered with debris.

The white sheets swimming limply just below the surface reflect more light and so catch the eye more than the other objects floating with them; they even stand out quite clearly against the general background, which is very dark. Not without some difficulty as a result of the eddies stirred up by my hand I catch hold of the nearest of these papers—a lot of identical rectangles probably from the same exercise book, the same packet, the same bundle— and note as I pull it out of the water, soggy and dripping, that they are printed pages torn from a book. The one I have fished out must be still legible, but there is not enough light to make out the tiny characters filling it in an almost uniform manner without any paragraphing.

I throw it back, a little farther out in the current, after crumpling it into a loose, sopping-wet ball that flattens out as it falls into the liquid mass with a faint, muffled *splosh*. I climb back up to the road, taking care not to slip on the narrow, uneven steps with their coating of very pale green, stringy weed growing less and less thickly as one rises above the level of movement in the water. I subsequently continue on my way through the dead city. Having gone to bed at an advanced hour of the night, I must then have slept for a very long time, as always.

I climb back up to the road by the little flight of slippery steps to get as close to the light as possible; right up against the cast-iron column of the electric street lamp, the old-fashioned ornamentation of which has already been described on several occasions, there is just enough of this for me to be able to make out the printed text, though with difficulty. I see from the very first sentences that the style is arid and somehow clumsy, like a word-for-word translation from a foreign language too different from our own. Having skimmed through it as quickly as the unfavorable conditions permit, I screw the wet sheet into a soft ball and throw it back into the water from on top of the quay. Leaning out over the edge of the sloping wall, I do not even hear it fall; the sound is lost amid all the after-rain noises that reach me from all sides as I return to my room along the avenue planted with ageless chestnut trees, my mind a blank, as always.

And now here is the text: I wake up, this must have been in winter, yet I slept with the casement wide open. It is morning, it is evening, I no longer know, and the uncertain light coming in from outside does nothing to clear up the point. I go over to the gaping window recess that looks out on the still-deserted avenue. Outside it is humid and mild. It must have been winter, I cannot say for certain on account of the dampness of the air, but at any rate there were no leaves left on the trees. Three or four stories below my window the bare black branches stand out with the precision of a diagram, as if drawn with india ink and a drawing pen, against a ground quartered by paving of perfect regularity (they are concrete slabs) across the whole width of the walkway along the bottom of the high, blind wall. I must have slept for a long time, a very long time probably, an indeterminate period, a blank. I remember nothing, as usual. I have an impression of having strolled through the old prison. There were pornographic inscriptions on the cell doors.

To get back here afterwards through the silent streets of the dead city I had to pass through a district littered with squalid rubbish, teetering walls, metal skeletons distorted by fire. Over vast areas the walls themselves had gone, probably blasted, and one was walking through debris between lines of iron girders still standing, supporting at only a few fragile points several levels of half-collapsed ceilings, their remains suspended in midair and flexing like tent canvas. Immediately afterwards came some ruined columns, arcades, and a sort of classical temple almost entirely preserved in its original state. Farther on, near a tangle of tubular structures from which still hung a red placard bearing the word *Information*, a veritable cataract pours from a gutted window to fall some fifteen meters onto what was left of the pavement, evidently as a result of a very large drain having sprung a leak in the upper stories of the building, or more likely of a water tank having burst. A man, a lone figure moving slowly forward through the wet rubble strewn all over the road, appears to be using a portable detector to follow some trace or other, his eyes glued to the needle of the counter.

And now comes the sound of footsteps, heavy, hurrying footsteps: several men wearing boots and running in fits and starts as if engaged in some breathless pursuit or playing a game. And afterwards the image of the eggs looms up: three white eggs on a white plate, each of the three ellipsoidal shells—uniformly mat and smooth—

touching the others at two points, though this makes only three points of contact in all. On the paving between the dead trees on the other side of the avenue there are now four or five men in track suits who appear to be dancing or possibly fighting with knives (in obedience to strict rules like those of fencing); a broad, short blade glints from time to time in one or other of their hands; it looks like one of the bayonet-knives used in the infantry, but in this case hidden up to the hilt in the sleeve of the jacket. Again the image of the eggs comes back, and the rapid sound of footsteps giving the impression of hampered, discontinuous flight; the shape and material of the three shells reproduce the model exactly, indeed the only thing that might arouse suspicion is their excessive perfection; but even so they are very lifelike eggs, hardly any bigger than real ones. Then a fresh figure in the ballet-fight emerges on the cross-ruled sheet with the simplified strictness of a diagram.

The image of the eggs yet again. . . . And immediately afterwards comes the explosion, looking in the dazzling white light like a radiant, frozen sun behind the trees.

II Ritual ceremony

In the little bare-walled room, now in semidarkness, the uncurtained window shows only the ruins silhouetted against the washed-out green of the sky. Still seated at her frail dressing table with the black-iron volutes that looks as if it had been drawn without the pen leaving the paper and that stands against the white wall just to the left of the recess, a very young girl holds herself motionless, perhaps on the alert for some suspicious sound in the menacing quiet of the huge house. She is listening. Her left hand is tucking a lock of her heavy, dull-golden hair over a delicately modeled ear while her right hand—the one holding the hairbrush—hovers at shoulder height in an interrupted movement: elbow bent, the oval of the brush with the soft black bristles offered upright, angling toward the rear a small mirror mounted on the back, its shape and its frame of dark wood reproducing on a smaller scale the oval looking-glass on the wall above the table.

And now, without either her head or her bust moving, the adolescent's bluish eyes leave the body of her companion, sprawled carelessly on the low divan in the darkened corner of the room behind her and reflected for her in the murky depths of the mirror. She shifts her attention to her own image, it too completely still, like a watercolor portrait in its frame: the fair hair, the large, staring eyes with the turquoise-gray irises, the parted lips, the round, very long neck, the bare chest, the young breasts with the perfect delineation of a diagram. She completes her suspended gesture, gently putting the brush down on the painted metal table, to the right of the china bowl, near the half-full glass that she now picks up and raises to her mouth in a very slow yet regular and continuous movement tracing a perfect curve; and, still gazing fixedly at herself in the oval mirror, she drinks.

Pale-lipped, she drinks the dark, blood-colored wine. Then she moves the glass away from her face, still with a residue of bright liquid in it, subsequently holding it near her breast with the small brown and pink areola, in approximately the same area of the picture as was occupied by the brush a moment ago but closer to her skin and just a little lower. A little lower still and more toward the back of the room the red stain on the floor has stopped growing; just on a level with the divan, some thirty centimeters beneath the limply flexed left knee of the young victim lying naked on her back among the fur cushions that lift up her hips and stomach, gaping thighs, and torn pubis, the red stain with the tortuous outline almost fills one of the white squares of the checkerboard and overflows into the adjacent black square, at least as far as the observer sitting motionless at her looking-glass is able to tell in the fading light. In the gathering dusk, and the resumption of calm, and already the advent of night, and drunkenness and terror, she listens.

She is listening to the murderer's footsteps on the stairs, the slow, heavy footsteps diminishing in volume stair by stair after walking away to the end of the interminable corridor off which the rooms lie behind a double row of identical doors, each coarse-grained wooden panel of boards that have come apart in several places as a result of the recent explosions presenting at eye level its little pinned-up rectangle of white card, on which has been painstakingly written in running hand the name—or rather the first name—of one or two inmates per cell.

Pressing one's body up against the double-locked door from inside, one can see thin vertical strips of empty space through the irregular cracks, but only directly in front of one, the thickness of the planks ruling out the slightest sideways glance toward either end of the corridor down which the footsteps always come, or alternatively go. So it would serve no purpose to turn, leave the iron chair by the window, and squeeze up to the gaps in the panel yet again in an attempt to witness the arrival on the landing of the celebrants of an indefinitely reiterated sacrifice, all this in the absurd hope of shortening the slow minutes before hearing the trampling of feet suddenly very close, the sounds of the big key being roughly inserted in the tiny hole, of the brutal crash of the lock—like a rifle being cocked—and of the sudden appearance in the cell of the man whose footsteps are as yet only distant creakings of wood right at the bottom of the great staircase.

Following their inexorable progress with an already hypertuned ear, the young prisoner slowly raises to her parted lips the heavy crystal glass that has just this minute been filled. She drinks. And the alcohol sinks its burning glow into her glazed limbs. Through murky layers of time and silence she listens to the murderer approaching, as he does every day at the same time, through the petrified house. Up he comes, floor by floor, crossing the successive landings one after another. He climbs the last flight, the last tread, at the top of the ancient oak staircase that reverberates beneath his boots. Afterwards his heavy step, though deadened slightly by the distance, makes a sharper sound on the paving of the corridor. Hands on the belt of his uniform tunic, he straightens the broad-bladed dagger now lying on the black and white marble floor at the foot of the divan, near the spreading red stain, in the bare room where the light is already going, the corners receding into darkness, the watchful girl still carefully brushing her long golden hair, her senses on the alert, her thoughts elsewhere.

But before he does anything else the man must enter the first room, the one with the word *Information* inscribed on a rectangle of white card slightly larger than the others. Inside it the four walls are entirely covered with oval portraits in mahogany frames—photographic enlargements in pastel tints looking like old-fashioned paintings—each of which shows an adolescent girl or very young woman with her hair down and her bodice wide open in order to expose her shoulders and chest; many of them are wearing thin chains around their necks with, suspended at their throats or between their breasts, a tiny gold cross. At the bottom of each frame is a name, a first name, written by hand on an ordinary gummed label; and two centimeters lower down an iron key for a large, antiquated type of lock hangs from a peg.

The visitor chooses a face with meticulous care, moving unhurriedly from one picture to the next. He stops at one and studies it at greater length: a pretty little redhead snatched from the nest for the luscious flavor of milk-white flesh in the best decorative tradition, green eyes wide with feigned surprise and a soft smile in which doubt is mingled with frailty, fear, and naive compliance, offering a pair of full, barely parted lips that have been chewed and moistened to make them shine more, all this

warmed-up intimacy as if suddenly surrendered to con-
cupiscent eyes, from the loose tawny curls in calculated
disarray to the two round breasts with points like pink
sweets that she dare not cover up by using her diffident
hands, which are joined by a rosary, to lift slightly and
with ostensible hesitation the froth of crumpled lace in
which they lie exhibited one beside the other like jewels in
a case. Having completed his inspection of these accumu-
lated signs and already savored their insistent adjectival
quality, the man spells out the name and unhooks the key.

He walks on down the corridor, stopping at each door
to read the name or names written on it, names taken from
flowers or from the virgin martyrs. On one of the doors
the handwritten letters have been crossed out several
times in red ink. The visitor pushes it open. The room is in
ruins; there is a gaping hole at least two meters across in
the shattered wall at floor level, opening without even a
temporary railing—of planks hastily nailed together or
stretched ropes—onto what is left of the street, which has
been three parts destroyed. An iron bed, its sheets in
disorder and stained with big red splashes, still stands
amid the rubble. Still hanging on a section of wall is the
oval painting representing some classical subject in which
a young girl pictured from the waist up, her large, wide-
open eyes staring into space without expression, without
seeing anything, is holding the point of a golden stylet to
her bare left breast just below the areola; the finely honed
tip of the blade must already have penetrated a little way
into the delicate, pearly skin, which has exuded a drop of
blood.

Still without the slightest movement of her porcelain
features, the girl again swivels her pupils, enlarged now by
the darkness, from the window, guarded on the outside by
five powerful wrought-iron bars between which can be

seen more clearly now against the orange-colored fringe of the opalescent sky the black silhouette of the captured city, not a single building of which appears to have been left intact, to the looking-glass, which throws back her own pale reflection, that curve of breast with its unavailing purity, and on the far right, at the center of the lighter cross formed on the russet furs by the spreadeagled body, the pattern, blurred now by darkness, of the oval bush offered up in sacrifice, its silky black fuzz split down the middle in a gash against which the drunken soldier crushes a bunch of purple grapes that burst and run down over the sensitive skin in a thick, vermilion liquid with a musky smell, a taste like iodine, and a slippery, viscid, unbearable sweetness. The girl's hand clenches in a spasm, then relaxes, suddenly quite limp, and loses its grip on the crystal glass, which drops and smashes on the black and white marble checkerboard into a thousand shimmering splinters.

III Landscape with cry

On the other side would be the window, it too fitted with a stout grating, looking out over the countryside, or at least over what is left of it: a gently undulating heath, which in this dull light looks iron-gray, crossed by lighter-colored paths tracing counter or parallel curves, lots of narrow, clearly drawn paths that form a whole network featuring multiple anastomoses and following a roughly east-west orientation, i.e., running from right to left.

In the distance, topping a more pronounced eminence, stands a ruined Graeco-Roman temple, the superstructure of an enormous underground building, now gone, that apparently occupied the whole of the shallow cone of the hill, with ramifications that are thought to have extended even deeper and farther out in all directions, the entire complex having been destroyed by being crushed from inside or at any rate sealed off by the vertical earthquake whose secondary volcanic thrusts then blocked all the exits with the exception of one staircase hollowed out of the white marble that still gives access to a kind of crypt where, legend has it, a sacrifice was made every evening to the god of pleasure, the victim being a young virgin (delicate features, long fair hair, flawless figure) selected from among the captives who had escaped the revels of the drunken soldiers, whose barbaric inventions are said to have stretched over a period of three days and three nights on the occasion of the sack of the city.

A black bull, supposedly representing the god, moves heavily over the cropped grass, muzzle aloft. Its eyes are bloodshot. Puffing from its dilated nostrils—twin jets of steam in the chilly air—is the spasmodic eruption of its breath, quickened as if by the rutting instinct or by anger. Suddenly its back curves forward and down, further accentuating the cruel character of the two sharp horns of a beast raised for the ring. One hoof fondles the soft ground with pent-up fury. Here their respective positions give the impression that the object of the animal's murderous rage is this abandoned car (a big white saloon, its battered, ruined bodywork a mess of rust and grease) sitting nose down in a pool of reddish mud in the right foreground.

On the other side, then, the room would look out over the criss-crossed lines of the goods station, now apparently no longer functioning as such. On the right, occupying the foreground, stands a tall, dead tree, unless it is simply that winter has stripped it of its leaves. Outlined among the bare branches—but this is probably a perspective effect—is a railway signal on its mast: a square of sheet metal divided into four smaller squares, two white and two red in an alternating, checkerboard pattern. Also visible in the vicinity are what look like long shreds of flimsy material, frayed with innumerable tears and stained with brownish spots, caught in the rigid twigs of the tree.

Just to the left, possibly waiting as a result of the signal having barred its progress, an extremely ancient black locomotive, streaked with rust, spits from its tall chimney spasmodic jets of white steam. Behind, extending to the extreme lateral edges of one's field of vision, there is nothing but deserted track, polished steel rails curving gently in parallel pairs to form a dense network of pale lines running from east to west at varying distances apart, joining up in places, then separating again, and ultimately all communicating with one another, in one place or another, by means of a complicated series of points.

Formerly commanding the entire system, a building constructed in wrought iron (its stiff, brittle, and at the same time contorted forms obviously dating from the end of the last century) occupies the rear of the scene, standing on a platform that, though not very high, is clearly distinguishable amid the general flatness. The building has extensive cellars, as witness the row of small oblong windows running the whole length of the façade at ground level; so low are these apertures that one is put in mind of horizontal loopholes, except that they are guarded by thick straight iron bars set upright and equidistantly and laying, for their part, no claim to any ornamental character whatsoever.

Moreover some of the underground rooms are even completely without ventilation from the outside, as, for example, the storeroom in which bottles of wine, neatly arranged in rows one on top of another, appear—in imitation of the labels one assumes they bear—to be themselves eaten away by a kind of gray leprosy under the action of which the regular pattern of the round bottoms of the bottles has virtually disappeared in some very badly affected areas, particularly toward the lower edge.

It is here amid the litter of glass and dusty cobwebs that the last murder was committed, or at least that a fresh victim was found, she too of unknown identity, her body run through in exactly the same fashion. Still lying on the dirt floor in the blackish layer of mingled clay and charcoal dust is a scrap of silk underwear, suspiciously stained, that the investigating authorities, having gone over the whole marshaling yard, put down in their report under the code name: Veronica's veil.

On the other side is the sea, smooth and gray, and the beach of fine-grained sand, it too quite flat and with not a person in sight. A vessel is lying offshore, its hull parallel to the water's edge (held in that position at the end of its anchor chain by some coastal current), its dark superstructure standing out against the toneless sky with great clarity despite the distance, as is often the case in wet, overcast conditions; one can even make out the barely concave lines of the cables linking bows and stern by way of the tops of the twin masts, outlining a sort of diagrammatic roof over the deck that embraces the davits, the hoists, the winches, the tall thin funnel, and the cube-shaped bridge house situated slightly forward.

There on the bridge a flashing red light that goes on and off at regular intervals—every two seconds—would be available with the naked eye to any attentive observer in the pale flush of dawn. It looks like an agreed signal communicating with the shore in connection with some imminent illegal unloading operation or furtive embarcation.

No one appears in response to this summons, however, along the whole length of the vast beach, the uniformity of which is broken only by, on the right, a piece of wreckage half buried in the sand: the black skeleton of an iron bed. Now either this is a freak of the receding tide or it is the abandoned evidence of a children's beach game: a pink and blond dressmaker's dummy, life-sized and with jointed limbs, a young woman made of flesh-colored plastic such as dress shops display in their windows, but in this case with no clothes on, is lying across the mattress of thin, interlocking strips of metal. One foot is hooked over (and tied to?) the uprights of the bedhead while the other leg, the bust, and the face with its immutable smile hang upside down on the smooth sand.

The absence of any prints around constitutes proof—supposing this to have been the work of children—that it antedates the last tide, which will have flowed and ebbed since. The long golden hair, floating in the ebb like limp seaweed, has frozen now in loose, straggly curls spread with careless abandon, heightening the impression of languor emanating from this topsy-turvy posture, the gaping thighs, the wide, upturned eyes, the open mouth with its sweet, vague smile, the limbs all adrift. One elbow is bent backwards; the other hand is stretched out, the tips of its tapering digits with their red-painted nails apparently trying to reach, as if it had been a lifebuoy, a second iron object only a short distance (barely twenty centimeters) away: the tall, rust-fretted wheel of a bicycle.

The tide seems to be coming in. The thin rollers of whitish foam are a little closer, a little more prominent, forming a whole moving network of more or less parallel lines in which unevennesses in the beach here and there give rise to curves and to shorter, slanting lines linking the long wavelets for a moment now and again as gradually these gain ground.

IV The excavations in retrospect

On the other side a child is looking out: a naked little boy moving toward the window that has neither curtains nor netting of any kind to obscure the crude pattern formed by the straight black lines of the uprights and rails dividing the aperture into six squares of coarse glass, smeared with the rain running down their dusty surfaces, here however still shiny in the indoor twilight of early morning or of a stormy late afternoon, between the high, frail-looking sewing machine (it is an old treadle-operated model) and the wardrobe with its looking-glass reflecting a jointed dummy, a young woman made of pink and blond plastic standing at the back of the room in a posture so inviting, despite a certain stiffness or fixity of gesture, that she seems—she too is nude—to be holding her arms out to the youngster coming toward her; but it is only toward her image as reflected in the greenish depths of the mirror, in other words in the opposite direction, that the little boy is moving—one hesitant foot still toeing the floor, reluctant to leave it altogether for fear of losing a precarious balance— away from the flesh-colored dummy, then, which instead of facing him is in fact behind him, turned as he is himself toward the white light of the window.

And now the wide-open window illuminates more clearly the receding lines of the floor, which look as if they continue vertically in the lower part of the window recess in a simple railing of parallel metal rods spaced about ten centimeters apart. On the other side of the silent avenue, behind the row of trees with their straight, parallel trunks and their bare black branches forming a loose, tangled web, stands the high, blind wall—enclosing a prison, or school, or barracks—with, visible above it, the top of a fairly long flat-roofed building, its façade of gaping apertures (all the woodwork has gone) completely encased in a crisscross of tubular scaffolding.

The interior of this building has already been described, with its long central corridor running the length of each floor and the rows of identical doors opening off it to right and left alternately. The present state of the premises hardly admits of speculation as to the use to which they may have been put, but most accounts include the episode of the adolescent girls (twelve in number, or a hundred and twenty, or possibly several thousands) in the traditional wedding dress of pure white tulle delivered up to soldiers in battle dress with, at their belts, protected by a leather sheath, the broad-bladed bayonet knife in use in the infantry; the heavy, low boots mentioned in this context are likewise—it should be said—infantry equipment. Another thing that very often crops up is the detail of the red pool spreading over the paved floor of the corridor, imperceptibly fed by a thick trickle meandering out of one of the rooms under the locked door.

By means, or not, of the rectangular trapdoor, which is fitted with a fat iron ring for lifting it (but this would certainly take several men), access is gained to the underground part of the building, unless this too is simply a fortified ground floor, because lateral openings as

narrow as loopholes and apparently admitting daylight
occur at regular intervals in the base of a shallow vault
forming the ceiling and sides of the hemicylindrical
gallery that occupies the entire length of the monument.
The floor of this is littered with rubble, piled up in heaps
so large as to raise the question of where the material
came from, since the vault itself seems to be virtually
intact. This must be the outcome not of dilapidations
connected with the recent events (the precise nature of
which has slipped my mind for the moment: bombardment, sack, earthquake?) but of much earlier archaeological excavations carried out lower down in the cellars, or
crypts, or catacombs, which in consequence would, this
time, be reached by the aforementioned trapdoor.

It is here in these basements, which are themselves on
several levels, that the celebrated "wall of vestiges" was
discovered, with the letter *H* made up of three wedge-
shaped impressions and the fresco known as "the
Caesarean," or at least what is left of it. Still visible a little
farther on are the site of the sacred stake for burnt
offerings, the collection of stones for ritual lapidations,
and the tube containing fourteen gold coins bearing the
changing effigy of Vanquished Vanadis. Finally a recently
uncovered bas-relief shows a girl kneeling on a socle,
hands behind her back and eyes blindfolded, surrounded
by less legible figures and with the word *INSEMINATIO*
incised above them. Examination of the west gable end
from outside reveals that the colossal chimney, the red-
brick stack of which occupies almost the entire width of
the virtually blind wall (there is one small square window
at the end of the top-floor corridor), must communicate
with the gigantic subterranean fireplace. Looked at from a
little farther away, from the beach in fact, down at the
edge of where the successive wavelets run out on the

smooth sand, the building looks like some nondescript provincial abattoir, the grim silhouette of which is sufficient on its own to make strollers turn away, so keeping deserted a huge area of the enormous beach where a completely naked little boy is playing solitary games with the industrial refuse washed up by the tide: an old truck tire, a bedstead with wrought-iron spirals welded to parallel rods, a life-sized, jointed dummy arranged in the manner described.

Let us also very quickly recall here: the sailing yacht, heeling over on a foam-flecked sea, its progress apparently arrested several cable lengths from the shore, delineated with a sharpness and delicacy that contrast with the sooty mass of an island breaking the line of the horizon farther back, its silhouette dominated by the shallow cone of a volcano trailing a plume of black smoke that likewise appears to hang motionless over the threatened city, a cluster of little whitish cubes rising in tiers around the lower slopes of a coastal hill that forms a headland, and finally the landing stage with its twisted piles supporting a gangway of disjointed planks running out toward the open sea between the hulls of vessels now reduced in greater or lesser degree to skeletons, mixed up with old car bodies, shreds of material, mutilated statues, domestic appliances eaten away with rust, sewing machine, wire mattress, or red umbrella no longer in use.

And now the dummy's face fills the whole window recess, where the iron balcony is built into a stout grating that blocks off the opening from top to bottom. The staring eyes, covered with a sort of binocular mask that looks as if it ought to blindfold them, are on the contrary able, thanks to this contrivance, to look simultaneously toward the interior of the room and in the direction of the avenue, along which the increasingly heavy car traffic is now flowing from right to left in a virtually continuous stream, producing a dull rumbling noise that is not unsuggestive of the sound of the sea before a storm: black limousines, all with identical bodywork, sweeping along at speed—instruments jammed on the flashing distress signal—without a road junction (are there any?) or traffic blockage to slow them down. Then comes the sudden silence, and the emptiness, as of water perhaps, again, quite calm.

Without going any closer to the gaping aperture, which contains neither railing nor casement (is he afraid of being seen or of losing his balance?), the child slowly opens his fingers to reveal the ball of paper he was hiding in the palm of his right hand, spends a moment longer in thought, unscrews the white, cross-ruled sheet, and re-reads the message: "After the vine harvest the threatened murderer will beware of the eggs of the bird that burns." To add more weight he drops in the little key with which he has just locked himself in the room, then refashions a nice compact ball around this core and throws it as far out as he can.

v A double-backed altar

It starts with a stone falling, in silence, vertically, motion-less. It is falling from a great height, an aerolith, a massive block of rock, compact, elongated, like a kind of giant egg with a lumpy surface.

Just below, on the smooth flat surface of the sea, the successive motionless fringes of foam form a series of horizontal lines running parallel to the straight edge of the long beach. It is hard to say on account of its no doubt considerable altitude whether the stone will end its fall on the pale brown sand or whether it will break the sheet of water, where its engulfment, once the showers of spray thrown up by the impact have fallen back, will leave only an indefinite series of concentric circles, again suspended in, for the time being, total fixity.

Fresh rose, flesh-colored, hanging upside down in the aperture of the wide-open window. . . . Abruptly shatter-ing the silence, a woman's cry rings out; the sound is very close, coming apparently from the next room, through what is probably a very thin partition wall; it is a young voice, clear, pure, and warm-toned, musical despite the violence of the yell (like a girl being stabbed), which dies away in a brief diminuendo. Bright flower, the color of a freshly opened wound. . . .

Or alternatively it was not through the partition wall but through the window, here too with both casements open on a white and blue sea. In the next-door room, which is like this one in every respect (this ponderous, rectangular building could be an isolated beach hotel built toward the end of the last century on the top of the moving dune whose gray lines stretch in both directions as far as the eye can see, a dangerous site that would explain the disturbing condition of its foundations and its cracked façade), like this room, then, as are all the other rooms whose identical doors, occurring at intervals that are equal though looking in perspective progressively shorter, line the left-hand side of the long and vertiginous corridor running from end to end of the hotel on each floor, from the great wooden staircase that used to be varnished to the narrow aperture (almost a loophole) right down there at the bottom of the opposite gable end, like it—I say—with perhaps one exception: that the fissures in the walls, which ramify into a complex network covering the whole surface of the plaster with its skin of wallpaper, the latter discolored and even torn at several points, here become, in places, proper crevices into which one could easily slip a knife blade. . . .

As I was saying: in the room next door, exactly opposite the open window recess that the axis of the outstretched body, were it to be produced, would bisect precisely, the murdered dressmaker's model is now lying on the long, white-painted wooden table—already described—that together with a nonmatching chair constitutes the entire furniture of this bare interior. Let us also swiftly recall the oval frame (without a picture) hung on the right-hand wall and the lines of the floor, their receding perspective apparently continued, right down there by the window, in the uprights of the railing silhouetted against the blue of the sparkling sea.

On the floor in the foreground stands an ancient phonograph with a flared bell, which must be just about contemporary with the sewing machine mentioned above and which with its horizontal horn also vaguely resembles it in shape. The stabbed body of the model was found on the beach, down at the edge of the dying wavelets, stripped naked, hands and feet chained to the bars of the makeshift bed (bier?): the iron skeleton, half-buried in the sand and eaten away by rust, of a shipwrecked vessel probably dating back a good way, judging from what has been said, as old at any rate as the sewing machine and the phonograph.

Right beside the latter (that is to say toward the back of the room) and almost touching the half-flung-back, blond head of the supine girl whose hair has come loose and hangs to the floor in rippling, seaweedy strands, a man who is not much older (being definitely under thirty) is leaning with one negligent hand on the back of the painted wooden chair; dressed entirely in black—patent-leather shoes, extremely formal double-breasted suit, and evening-dress tie—gloved, and wearing a bowler hat, he appears to be dreaming on his feet. His figure is tall and slim, his features regular and finely formed. This may be the murderer, although he bears a bewildering re-semblance, both facially and in terms of dress, to the two plainclothes policemen waiting for him behind the door, out in the corridor.

The three of them, frozen in similar postures, ears cocked in the same fashion, are listening to the victim's cry as recorded on the wax cylinder, which perfectly reproduces its every modulation. If the presumed criminal has his head inclined a little more to one side it is the better to catch the last vibrations of the voice as they emerge from the horn with the flared bell that stands at his feet. Since he has his back to the window he has not yet seen the female figure who has just appeared in the aperture, behind the balcony. Smiling, dressed in a filmy beach robe of white tulle, as was the fashion at the period, and wearing a translucent sunbonnet, she it is, then, who has in her left hand, holding it by the end of the thorny stem, a red rose whose half-open corolla hangs head down just above knee height.

One is of course immediately struck by the idea that the newcomer could be Lady H-G. in person and that the two adolescents in the room are her own children, the fraternal twins David and Vanessa: the girl still with her light golden hair haloing her large, pale blue, swimming eyes, and the boy whose incestuous and subsequently fratricidal desires came to light at an extremely tender age, as has been mentioned on several occasions here and there.

There is something wrong, however, in that the difference in age between the precocious murderer and his young mother with the figure of a classical statue appears at first sight to be too small. Shelving this detail for the moment, let us first itemize the principal exhibits that are beyond discussion. Two of these can be seen in the hands of the policemen mounting guard by the closed door, one on the right and the other on the left, namely, the fishing net with the large square mesh in which the graceful body of Vanessa was imprisoned, like some siren taken by surprise, and brought to the surface by a fisherman dredging for shellfish, and secondly the large skittle pin of turned wood ringed with numerous projections, some

crueler than others, said to have been used to deflower
her. Each of the other clues gathered from the text, placed
directly on the floor of broad, receding boards, occupies
one of the empty rooms lining the corridor: the falling
stone, the glass of wine (adulterated, to all appearances),
the flesh-colored rose with the scarlet heart, etc.

One preliminary conclusion asks to be drawn: the
episode that goes by the name of "the difficult crossing"
would in this case contain a double allusion, to the sinister
vessel on board which the young girl was dragged by her
ravishers, and to the crime that awaited her there before
she was thrown into the sea. Second (hypothetical)
remark: this same phallus-shaped wooden object may
have been used as a club by the young man's accomplices
during the brief ensuing struggle, in the course of which
David was apparently hurt; the small red wound on his
temple at the corner of the right eye would be the outward
sign of this, soon to leave no more trace than a tiny scar,
whereas the total loss of memory on the murderer's part
would indicate a more permanent inner trauma.

There is no point in going over the story of the ship
again, which has already been related at ample length, nor
over the rape proper (or the metaphorical image of the
bleeding flower); on the other hand, it seems to me
extremely important to recall without delay the reek of
seaweed all through the hotel, the iodic, sweetish
pungency of which is beginning to go to my head. I open
the next door: this room is completely unoccupied, empty,
abandoned. . . . But isn't this the one that a moment ago
contained the dark wine with the suspicious color? Now,
though, behind the railing in the open window, there are
these busts of men in black suits, several compact rows of
them, all turned toward me, their expressions similarly
fixed: onlookers, probably, attracted by the sudden cry to

the immense beach, which a moment ago was deserted, as was pointed out in the appropriate place. I shut the door in a hurry. In the room that follows there are again the three white eggs, intact, nestling together in a little glass bowl set (by whom?) on the ledge of the gaping window recess.

I see immediately that this is a trap: if I pick up one of the eggs (for example, to examine more closely whether it does not bear some telltale sign on its shell) I break the closed circuit passing through the three tangential points, so triggering the explosion that is to set fire to the building and complete its destruction. I then hear footsteps in the corridor. I turn around. It's the doctor already, come no doubt to make the official report, with his bowler hat and his little black bag marked with a golden caduceus and using the other hand to make measured, as it were circumspect, signs, apparently in response to certain welcoming gestures, seeking to calm their excessive exuberance, the gestures, it goes without saying, being absent.

I for my part confine myself to nodding him a brief greeting as he passes. Then, without thinking, I glance behind me—to note with surprise that he too has turned around, having even halted after a few steps to examine me at greater leisure. In my confusion, and in an attempt to put a good face on things as quickly as possible, I grasp the knob within reach of my hand—or almost—in order to open another door, but this time one in the right-hand wall of the long corridor. Is this the first exit available on this side? I do not recall, at any rate, having noticed any others previously. . . .

A fresh incident prevents me from devoting my attention to this problem: having suspended my projected door-opening with a mechanical movement in order to look yet again at the palm of my hand, as if the white china knob may have left some mark on it, I become aware of the real cause—which is quite different—of this apparent change of plan: the knob turned, but the door resisted. I put off this pointless examination of my digits until later. No time to dwell on. . . . I give the knob a shake. The door is closed (aha!) beyond any possibility of error. I then notice the small shiny key still in the keyhole. It feels hot to the touch, curiously enough, which does not prevent the lock from functioning normally, quite the contrary perhaps, aha!

Inside it is very dark. I enter on tiptoe. I am in time for the beginning of the performance. Taking endless precautions in order not to disturb my neighbors, I sit down noiselessly in a seat upholstered in red velvet that has been left vacant at the rear of the box. Unfortunately I do not have a very good view of the stage between the dark heads of the spectators sitting in front of me, who, having turned around for a moment at my late arrival, are now back in their normal positions. By contorting my neck as best I can, however, I am at last able to make out a kind of open-air fireplace with an adolescent couple kneelng in front of it. Aha! This gives me enough to know that the opera being performed this evening is entitled *The Idol*, contrary to what was announced by the posters outside. As I know the piece by heart (and for good reason!), I settle myself more comfortably in my seat for a bit of peaceful reflection.

A short while later, my eyes having grown used to the darkness, I notice beside me a frail-looking blonde who is making fruitless efforts to see something of the performance by shifting from side to side on her velvet seat. Making a pretext of the "excuse me" that I addressed to her before when I had accidentally touched her on entering the box, I decide to help her out of her difficulty by murmuring in her ear a brief résumé of the plot, which recounts—I tell her—a little-known version of the Phoenix legend: the egg, in exploding, has given birth to a large black bird whose winged form emerges from the flames. It flies over the sea, this at great length, then over the cliffs.

Scrutinizing the ground with its piercing gaze, it finally discovers what it was looking for: a woman's high-heeled shoe lying among the rocks, the only relic washed up by the waves after the engulfment of the bather (mentioned already) and her scanty clothing. The moment the bird lands on it the shoe catches fire of course and immediately becomes an enormous pyre. By degrees everything is involved in the blaze (which explains among other things the abnormal temperature of the little key), right down to the brass section of the orchestra. Vanessa appears (wearing on this occasion, I have forgotten why, a raven-black wig), she too in search of the precious lost shoe. Now she only has to swallow the bird. Since the bird has meanwhile had time to lay another (parthenogenetic) egg, the permanence of the cycle is assured. . . .

Here my listener seems to have been suddenly taken ill, as if my words—which she was drinking in avidly—had been poisoned. To the accompaniment of disapproving shushing noises from my neighbors, who have turned around again, I carry the unconscious girl to a little room of whose existence I know (though not its function, which is ill defined) not far from there, on the other side of the corridor serving the boxes. I lay the limp body on the rectangular table, which is covered with a thick red velvety material (a gaming table, possibly?). But the stranger's intricate hairdo has come undone on the way and her heavy blond hair now hangs down to the ground, which has the advantage of bringing us back to a situation that has already been itemized (under the scarlet cloth the wood is sure to be painted white). Moreover the doctor in the long black coat makes an extremely timely entrance. Without saying a word he opens his leather bag and lays out his instruments in order to make an immediate injection in the milk-white skin of his lovely patient, whom closer observation reveals to be very much less diaphanous than she had looked to me in the semidarkness of the auditorium, where the only light came from one distant, lurid source: the sacred brazier at the very back of the stage.

To get rid of my scanty clothing and delicate evening shoes I unthinkingly throw them out of the window, which is open wide on the darkness and the murmur of the ocean. A short while later (how long?) I am again walking in the mild, humid night between the tall rows of façades whose dilapidated condition has been pointed out already, I no longer remember in what connection; some are even so ruined as to make it hard to imagine how normal domestic life can still carry on behind such a succession of disturbingly creviced walls, bricked-up windows, gaping slits, and dislodged cornices from which some dangerous block of stone might at any moment become detached.

Freshly washed, almost spruce, having held its own as if by a miracle in the midst of this demolished quarter, I notice yet again the little shop selling first-communion and wedding dresses, whose signboard saying "Vanities Divine" has so far lost only one of its letters.

Description of the windows, the white tulle dresses, the dummies, the trying-on cubicle, the double back and how it works, etc. This whole passage is already pretty familiar. Possibly, however, there is still one detail worth noting: leaving the Municipal Theater right in the middle of the performance, I crossed the broad, dark, empty plaza in which, beneath the yellow light of one of the few lampposts, stood a wooden table covered with a sort of cloth that hung low on all four sides; it must have been the stall of some fruiterer or drinks seller, the reddish stain marking one of the edges of the rectangle looking as if it had been made by juice of some kind—pomegranate or watermelon—or alternatively by wine. A rustic stool beside it, consisting simply of a slice from a tree trunk mounted on four crude legs, put one in mind of a meat-block.

As I was afterwards crossing the old bridge over the dark river, its still, taut surface marbled here and there by gleaming eddies, its rate of flow accelerated by the spate that has brought its level up to the vaults of the arches, a girl of about twelve, a hawker wandering the deserted evening streets on the unlikely chance of finding a late stroller, came up to me and offered me the last rose from the tray slung at her stomach. I paid the small price asked for but did not want to take the flower, suddenly experiencing violent repulsion at the mere thought of touching it. Reaching the other end of the bridge, I heard a muffled sound behind me as of a large stone dropping from a great height into the river.

Another outstanding problem would be that of the empty frame, which must be directly related to the little key, a hidden link that would doubtless call for extensive reasoning. But I must push on, having wasted enough of the limited time at my disposal in descending the slippery steps to the water's edge, groping in the deceptive shadows that move incessantly within the darkness, in order to wash my hands as best I can in the current. I immediately come upon this uncertain, absent place with its succession of demolition sites, patches of waste ground, tall fences occasionally concealing the bases of dispropor-tionately large, frail, provisional-looking metal structures, derelict buildings, wooden huts, and, farther on, this huge excavation in which, right down at the bottom—the distance making them look ridiculous—machines are moving about, apparently probing with their headlights for remains of some civilization buried at an unusual depth. . . . Nor do I stop at the chestnut-lined avenue bordering the prison, already described.

So now here I am, alone in the gray light of early dawn, in front of my own window, which is still open, waiting for me, in the middle of a façade most of which has been bricked up. A large mirror occupying all the wall visible behind the table (still the same one) reflects the bluish image of the house opposite as if the outside of the room were the inside, following an arrangement not unsuggestive of the fanatic temple of which I am laboriously reconstructing the plan day after day, through repetitions, contradictions, and omissions.

CODA

It's that same cry again: a yell possibly of terror, or of acute pain, or of feverish agitation; somewhere very close the same long-drawn-out, searing cry, quickly dying away as a distant groan, suddenly pierces the night and the silence. Sitting up in bed with a start, supporting myself on both arms held out behind me amid a tangle of damp sheets, head cocked, ears straining, I listen to the silence, again, falling back.

I listen to the nagging chatter of the jays in the ever-present forest and the thud of the axes in the bottom of my chest, attacking at its base the trunk of a still gigantic tree. Who was it saying—I remember now—that there was no forest, no jays probably or was it woodpeckers, and no dogs? The vast, abandoned forest completely surrounds the impossibly large dwelling that stands there empty, beset up to its topmost windows by foliage crowding the window recesses, shifting, rustling, beating at the panes like some sly sea alive with adjectives and metaphors, poised to swallow you up. In the great empty house, once peopled room by room, floor by floor (including, indeed principally, the attics and cellars), peopled—I remember

now—by the convenient theory of small minor deities, I
wind my spiraling way in search of . . .

Tiny butterflies in fragile plumage dancing over the tall
grass with no aim and no past in the rays of the setting
sun. Or alternatively, still frail and pink, starfish languishing on the wet sand where day after day the ebbing tide
abandons them to tender death. It was yesterday already,
so remote.

It was yesterday. And the barely perceptible smile of
the silent moth hunter, not a line of whose face moves as
his pale eyes, keeping a sharp lookout beneath the torpor
of the long hours of adolescence, are motionless as they
follow the whimsical little victims flitting inquisitively
around him. . . . His crepe soles make no sound—already
mentioned, as I recall—his movements are soft, measured,
an apparently dreamy quality masking the precision, the
violence that will suddenly overtake the one that, for a
moment, alights. . . .

Motionless forever. There was blood under the half-
open door, already been said, already been said, and a
high-heeled shoe of sky-blue leather lying where the last
wave had dropped it amid the festoons of wrack marking
the top of the tide. Once more I move forward, counting
my steps. It is important not to alarm the lazy young
vanessa pretending to be asleep. And the movements are
as if imagined, etched in solitude, absence, that caught the
creature in the meshes of the invisible net; or rather would
have caught. . . .

Now the red pool is spreading over the checkered
paving of the long corridor where it shines with a bright
gleam in the semidarkness; its irregular, sinuous edge,
which follows exactly the shape of the depressions in the
floor, delineating curves at successive levels, now looks as
if it is on the point of reaching the delicate abandoned

slipper lying on its side in the middle of a black square, left there in the panic of flight or equally perhaps kicked there accidentally by a nonchalant heel on returning very late from the theater, during one of those hasty, half-conscious undressing operations when one's eyes are already beginning to close. The little iridescent goddesses make such unexpected, rapid movements that one barely sees their transformations take place, as if they had passed without transition from one costume to the other, from a light dress to a total absence of dress or of any undergarment, from one posture of their slender bodies to another posture, again frozen.

But the collector of precious butterflies, delicate, silky creatures that they are, knows that if he wants nothing but absolutely new specimens it is better to take the chrysalis in order to have it emerge under cover and catch it before it can run the risk, by knocking itself in one place or another, of damaging its wings; then to sacrifice the captive without delay on the altar of Voluptuous Vanadis (also known as the Vampire Vanadis), at first by means of the various drugs laid down in the Code of Venoms, finally impaling the virgin belly alive on an erect needle, which to the victim is as big as a broad-bladed sword or long dagger.

And the blood runs in a vermilion rivulet that will soon pass through the dark chink beneath the ill-fitting door, etc. A quick gust of warm wind and the little wave again breaks on the wet sand of the beach, leaving exposed in its wake the fresh shellfish in lustrous flesh tones that glint for a brief moment in the blazing light amid the few scraps of kelp with their odor of iodine, salty and with a hint of musk, and the svelte starfish with limbs awry, lying sweetly open in every direction.

But again the wavelet breaks, carrying everything off

with it: the blond strands of seaweed smelling of iodine, the bloodstains, the delicate evening shoes, the cries of the gulls. And I move on, yet again, faced with the row of closed doors, down the endless empty corridor, unalterably neat and clean.

Selected Grove Press Paperbacks

E237   ALLEN, DONALD M. (Ed.) / The New American Poetry: 1945-1960 / $3.95

B181   ANONYMOUS / A Man With A Maid / $1.95

B334   ANONYMOUS / My Secret Life / $2.45

B155   ANONYMOUS / The Pearl / $1.95

B383   ARSAN, EMMANUELLE / Emmanuelle II / $1.95

E425   BARAKA, IMAMU AMIRI (LeRoi Jones) / The Baptism and The Toilet / $2.45

E96   BECKETT, SAMUEL / Endgame / $1.95

B78   BECKETT, SAMUEL / Three Novels (Molloy, Malone Dies, The Unnamable) / $1.95

E33   BECKETT, SAMUEL / Waiting For Godot / $1.95

B79   BEHAN, BRENDAN / The Quare Fellow and The Hostage: Two Plays / $2.45

B186   BERNE, ERIC / Games People Play / $1.95

B386   BERNE, ERIC / Transactional Analysis in Psychotherapy / $1.95

E417   BIRCH, CYRIL WITH KEENE, DONALD (Eds.) / Anthology of Chinese Literature, Volume 1: From Early Times to the Fourteenth Century / $4.95

E584   BIRCH, CYRIL (Ed.) / Anthology of Chinese Literature, Volume 2: From the 14th Century to the Present Day / $4.95

E368   BORGES, JORGE LUIS / Ficciones / $2.95

B283   BRAUTIGAN, RICHARD / A Confederate General From Big Sur / $1.50 (also available as E478 / $1.95)

B120   BRECHT, BERTOLT / Galileo / $1.95

B108   BRECHT, BERTOLT / Mother Courage and Her Children / $1.50

B333   BRECHT, BERTOLT / The Threepenny Opera / $1.75

B115   BURROUGHS, WILLIAM S. / Naked Lunch / $1.95

GT422   CLURMAN, HAROLD (Ed.) / Seven Plays of the Modern Theater / $4.95 (Waiting For Godot by Samuel Beckett, The Quare Fellow by Brendan Behan, A Taste of Honey by Shelagh Delaney, The Connection by Jack Gelber, The Balcony by Jean Genet, Rhinoceros by Eugene Ionesco and The Birthday Party by Harold Pinter)

E190   CUMMINGS, E.E. / Selected Poems / $1.95

E344	DURRENMATT, FRIEDRICH / The Visit / $2.95
B342	FANON, FRANTZ / The Wretched of the Earth / $1.95
E130	GENET, JEAN / The Balcony / $2.95
E208	GENET, JEAN / The Blacks: A Clown Show / $2.95
B382	GENET, JEAN / Querelle / $1.95
B306	HERNTON, CALVIN C. / Sex and Racism in America / $1.95
E101	IONESCO, EUGENE / Four Plays (The Bald Soprano, The Lesson, The Chairs, and Jack, or The Submission) / $1.95
E259	IONESCO, EUGENE / Rhinoceros and Other Plays / $1.95
E216	KEENE, DONALD (Ed.) / Anthology of Japanese Literature: From the Earliest Era to the Mid-Nineteenth Century / $4.95
E573	KEENE, DONALD (Ed.) / Modern Japanese Literature / $4.95
B300	KEROUAC, JACK / The Subterraneans / $1.50
B9	LAWRENCE, D. H. / Lady Chatterley's Lover / $1.95
B373	LUCAS, GEORGE / American Graffiti / $1.50
B146	MALCOLM X / The Autobiography of Malcolm X / $1.95
B326	MILLER, HENRY / Nexus / $1.95
B100	MILLER, HENRY / Plexus / $2.95
B325	MILLER, HENRY / Sexus / $2.95
B10	MILLER, HENRY / Tropic of Cancer / $1.95
B59	MILLER, HENRY / Tropic of Capricorn / $1.95
E636	NERUDA, PABLO / Five Decades: Poems 1925-1970 / $5.95
E359	PAZ, OCTAVIO / The Labyrinth of Solitude: Life and Thought in Mexico / $3.95
E315	PINTER, HAROLD / The Birthday Party and The Room / $1.95
E411	PINTER, HAROLD / The Homecoming / $1.95
GT614	POPKIN, HENRY (Ed.) / Modern British Drama / $5.95 (A Taste of Honey by Shelagh Delaney, The Hostage by Brendan Behan, Roots by Arnold Wesker, Serjeant Musgrave's Dance by John Arden, One Way Pendulum by N. F. Simpson, The Caretaker by Harold Pinter and essays by major British directors and playwrights.)
B202	REAGE, PAULINE / The Story of O / $1.95
B323	SCHUTZ, WILLIAM C. / Joy / $1.95
B313	SNOW, EDGAR / Red Star Over China / $3.95
B319	STOPPARD, TOM / Rosencrantz and Guildenstern Are Dead / $1.95
E219	WATTS, ALAN W. / The Spirit of Zen: A Way of Life, Work, and Art in the Far East / $2.45

GROVE PRESS, INC., 196 West Houston St., New York, N.Y. 10014